The Penitent's Rose

A collection of short stories on guilt

To Molly & Asif,
A guilty Pleasure...
Henry Bewley

HENRY JOHN BEWLEY

CONTENTS

FOREWORD

1. MAPMAKER   1
2. I AM NOT HERE   10
3. MR DECUERVO   23
4. ALBERT CLOCK   30
5. ONE POUND AND ONE SHILLING   38
6. KILL VERONICA POUND!   48
7. TRANSMISSION   54
8. LETTERS FOR MONIQUE   64
9. HABIT   72
10. THE PLANET HAS LIMITS   78
11. NEW BEGINNING   84
12. TIME TRAVEL   88
13. *COOL* BRITANNIA   106
14. LIFE AFTER DEATH   118
15. READY?   128
16. FLAT BREAD   135
17. NO TOAST   139
18. BREAKFAST WITH SONIA   146

19. MESMERISING   152

20. STARBUCKS   159

21. POP-UP SADNESS   167

22. WE ARE SO MUCH MORE CIVILIZED   170

23. MEN ARE SO DIFFERENT, AREN`T THEY?   176

24. CHÂTEAU DE MARVILLE   186

25. TIT FOR TAT   190

26. TALL BOY   195

27. CROSSRAIL   206

28. ROUTEMASTER   210

29. TAKEAWAY FOREVER LIFE   215

30. FUNNYMAN   220

31. SERVING KATE   226

32. I DIDN'T RECOGNISE HIM   231

33. DRINK, FOR TOMORROW WE DIE   239

34. MAGUS   243

35. THEY ONLY WANT ONE THING   253

ACKNOWLEDGEMENTS

ABOUT THE AUTHOR

FOREWORD

The crocus is one of the first flowers to bloom after winter. Spring bringing rebirth to nature. As a representation of renewal, the spring crocus linked with purging after wrongdoing, has been called the penitent's rose. A flower to give hope to the guilty, as it symbolises a possibility of healing. One of the ways this is possible is through the creation of art. Albert Camus wrote: *A guilty conscience needs to confess. A work of art is a confession, and I must bear witness.*

I have been a writing for many decades. My creative writing started as therapy: I needed to better understand myself. Using highly autobiographical stories, I was able to express stuff about myself in a 'fictional' format. There was catharsis from tackling disturbing memories and feelings – getting it all out! As the years passed, a joy of telling a story took over from personal reflection. I came to find pleasures in writing fiction. When there is a creative flow, writing can come easy and give a sense of well-being. Moving characters around in a space is fun, analogous to playing in a doll's house. I developed my writing method and craft. There is now a sense of accomplishment in a job completed and done well.

During the Covid-19 pandemic I was motivated to push my work forward, both novel-length work-in-progress and short story projects. I had already written frequently on guilt, in its many different forms. It is a theme that has kept featuring in my work, from the very start. Guilt was an important emotion during the pandemic as people were forced to make difficult choices. Every day, we were confronted with many types of guilt – our own 'was I being careful enough' or 'could I do more for the community' and for others who 'broke the rules' or live with the thought that they 'may have infected someone else.' Sometimes there is no right answer. Even though I knew my dad in his care home needed visits to keep his spirits up, I felt guilty for travelling from my home to see him as we were all being encouraged to stay home. I also felt guilty for not visiting frequently enough. Every decision, mine and others', could be criticised. Guilt was everywhere. I realised that there were many more stories on guilt that I wanted to write. That inspired me to produce new stories.

Tackling the issue of guilt in this collection is coming full circle in my writing. I return to a subject from my first motivation to write, a way towards healing, but now in fiction. To me, each story is like a spring crocus (the penitent's rose). In a sense, I examine (and try to purge) guilt. This collection contains thirty-five of my favourite pieces.

'The Penitent's Rose' could easily have never been published. At the start of 2024, I had a massive heart attack and a quadruple bypass. It is only out, this spring, because I have survived - perhaps for my own renewal?

Anyway, as a map can be useful to help navigate, we start with the story: A Mapmaker. The main character, Lazlo, and I both try to share any interesting patterns we notice in life.

Henry John Bewley

1. MAPMAKER

Lazlo leaned over his raised drafting table to carefully align a blank sheet of paper. He was excited as he had defined the subject of a new concept: some sort of triangulation to represent the Holy Trinity. He started, as he usually started, by delicately applying a black border line. He thought: *I was chosen, in childhood, for showing special insight; when taught of Heaven and reincarnation, I asked: 'How can both be true?' Years of training followed.*

On hearing his shop's bell tinkling, he looked up, over his glasses. A mousy-haired young man wearing a trench coat entered. The fine border line needed a little time to dry anyway.

Lazlo made his way to stand behind his shop counter, to the right of the drafting table. He took his metal-framed glasses off his nose and let them drop and dangle on their string, around his neck. He waited. After the customary few minutes to show politeness, he asked: 'Good afternoon. Can I help you, sir?'

'I'm looking for a map to help my decision-making,' the young man hesitated, 'to make the way in front of me more of a clear road. Life is a journey after all, isn't it?'

'Indeed, sir. If only we were all the same and the purpose of every man's life simple … The map you seek can only be understood at its end.'

'Are you making fun of my youth?' He'd raised his voice.

'Oh no, sir. All human beings start at different places and travel through different lands. I can show you the map of my journey, so far. But I cannot make a map to help you on the journey you have yet to embark upon.' A good mapmaker had to be honest.

The young man's face dropped. Lazlo knew his words had disappointed him. He moved from the counter to the oak round table in the centre of the shop. He pushed aside a large dusty vellum chart and searched under a pile of sky-coloured maps. 'I believe I have something Maya Blue here, that might be of interest to you, sir.'

Lazlo heard his shop's bell tinkling – the young man had walked out of the shop. Being as honest as possible does not make a good salesman.

He moved back to his drafting table to work on his new idea. He wondered: *Rather than representing what is already clearly apparent, can I identify the new commonalities and relationships between our different religions and map them?* He picked up a small pot of iron gall ink for its permanent deep blue-black colour. His choice of pen came, as second nature, down to the nib that gave him the exact width of line he wanted.

He drew a bold baseline straight across the centre of the paper. *A commonality is that everyone wants to be told what they want to hear –*

I know this to be true. He drew a second line at 45°, with passion, moving to the left from the baseline. *It feels bad to think we turn to dust so we make up stories of an afterlife.* The third line was at 45°, it moved to the right from the baseline. *It is difficult to accept we live in a chaotic world so we are drawn to stories that suggest order.* While the fourth line was at 90°, straight upwards from the baseline. *No one wants to feel they are alone.*

He looked at what he had drawn – a simply representation of uncertainty as uncomfortable. There was nothing to show anything informative about the Holy Trinity. Unhappy with his initial attempt, he screwed up the paper, stirred his ink and started again.

*

An hour later, the little bell rang out again. Lazlo was already standing behind his shop counter.

A man wearing white ceremonial robes entered the shop, walking with the aid of a fine-looking cane; a waft of incense followed.

Lazlo made sure he gave no indication that he had instantly recognized this man of God. He had heard of Provini's recent bereavement so he knew, for him, white would be the colour of mourning. For Lazlo, white was the philosopher's wool; he had seen alchemists burn zinc to form the woolly tufts of white residue needed for the paint.

'I would like to buy a map,' said Provini.

Lazlo looked into a face that had recently been weeping. 'You've come to the right place.'

'Good.' Provini picked up one of the sky-coloured maps from the oak table and unfolded it while looking at another map on wall.

What could he be looking for amongst those maps – perhaps a new country to forget the difficult land he currently inhabits? Lazlo moved towards his customer. 'That's Africa, sir.'

Provini put the map in his hand down unseen.

'It is maps and charts that mould our view of the world, sir.'

'All right.'

'A map's design is chosen, sir, by a mapmaker.'

'Very good …'

'I have maps showing beer vs wine, pasta vs rice vs grain cultures …' As Provini showed no interest, Lazlo changed tack and pointed to a map on the wall in three colours – reddish-brown, yellow ochre and ultramarine, but mostly ultramarine; a map by Lazlo Pelagatti [Ph.D. in the Cartography of Meaning, Prague University]. 'Take this. I divided the world into three categories. Africa and Asia are mainly reddish-brown as they are honour/shame cultures. The few fear/power cultures are shown in yellow ochre. While we in Europe and much of the Americas are coloured ultramarine to represent our guilt/innocence culture. By that I mean, everyone is obsessed with right and wrong, justice, the protection of innocence and the avoidance of guilt.'

'I am in pain. You may have heard of me? Luca Provini. My wife …'

'I'm sorry sir, I —'

'I am so lonely. I am stumbling around in the dark. Have you a map to show me a way out of pain?'

'An unusual request.'

'Anything that could help?'

'I once tried to make a universal map of grief. I talked to so many sad people to research it but it came to nothing – nothing worked. Everyone's journey is different.'

'I don't know what's going on. I'm going around and around in circles and getting nowhere.'

'I'm not sure my maps will be able to —'

'I heard about you. There seems to be a unity between us. We both look for the truth in the world.'

'Yes, in my work I seek the truth but it is a quest not a destination.' Lazlo paused, expecting Provini to respond. He didn't, forcing Lazlo to continue. 'I guess we both strive for understanding. I don't have any specific answers. But I have followed my own path and seen some patterns … I try to conceptualise knowledge in my maps. The people who buy my maps tell me they are unique.'

'I've been told your projections could help me … They have their own power?'

'Umm, yes, but I don't think in the way you are —'

'Are there incantations put over them?'

'No, you have the wrong idea … I do have a special supply of paper, pens and ink.'

'But, there is sorcery in the symbols that you use?'

'No … No sorcery.'

'I heard you had things … exotic? Something that could

relieve my grief?'

Lazlo was pleased the conversation about sorcery had ended. He pointed to the back of the shop. 'Through here, sir.' He escorted Provini behind a curtain to the small rectangular back room.

Inside, Lazlo immediately began to tidy up. On the left-hand side of the room, he pushed a deep drawer closed into its long cabinet full of drawers. He moved to fold-up two maps laid out on the table that stretched the full length of the wall on the right. Lazlo noted a little green on the back of the first. He was quick in his folding to hide the discolouration. When done, he added it to a pile of folded maps also on the table.

The last remaining unfolded map was a representation of a naked man with stars and lines all over him. Provini picked it up. 'And what have we got here?'

'That is a projected body map. We all have one of those in our head.'

'Interesting.' Provini put down the map. 'Who drew these maps?'

'Everything in this shop was drawn by myself. All the maps come from my —'

'Good. Good.'

Lazlo felt he had to say more. 'Every map shows something about the maker's perception of the world ... I like to think my customers come back as they are assured of my trustworthiness.'

Provini gave no verbal response. In the quiet that followed, he casually picked up the projected body map, folded it to a booklet shape, then held on to it as he continued to look around.

Lazlo's hopes for a sale rose. The maps were not cheap. Anything above a dozen sales was a good week.

He knew sometimes it was best to allow his customer to browse. He waited a minute before he unfolded a map from the pile on the table. 'If you are looking for a diversion ... This shows the preference for different sexual positions by geography.'

Provini's face reddened.

Lazlo refolded the map, picked up another and unfolded that. *He asked for relief from his grief, Body parts men desire will surely distract.* 'Here ... this picture, of a woman on her side, sets out a breakdown of male desire to the different body parts. As you can see, the most common are face, pudenda, breasts, buttocks, leg, hair, feet and toes ... The more exotic like nails, necks and ears. Then there are those, in small numbers, with a taste for the body fluids or body odours.'

'I don't know why —' A vein on Provini's neck began pulsing.

'True, there are many fetishes not focused on the body at all but directed towards an object. I found out the most common are a liking for underwear, footwear and skirts. But I could not map this subject. The list is endless as it is so subjective ...'

Provini's face was red with anger. 'I asked for something to relieve my grief and you —'

'I see you have picked up ...' Lazlo moved a hand towards the folded map in Provini's hand. 'Let me see ...'

Provini handed it over. Lazlo recognised the map but put on

his glasses, just in case, to read the cover. 'This is a projection of our ghost emotions.'

'I don't understand.'

'In this map, I tried to capture … no that's not the right word for it … I tried to know the emotions that live on after … The feelings we have for people who don't exist any more but were important?' Lazlo recognised how insensitive his words were only after he had spoken.

Provini shook as if holding back tears. He was clearly still grief stricken. 'No. I don't —'

Lazlo tried to redirect his explanation by offering clarification in general terms. 'It projects on to the Cosmos … like the great deities.'

'Are you saying God, Our Father, and Mother Earth are projections?'

'No … well, maybe, the projections that live on are something like that. We understand the world through our mothers and fathers and we project back on to the Cosmos our parental figures —'

'That is sacrilege!'

'We are created by them. We create out of —'

Provini banged the end of his stick down onto the ground, turned and walked toward the shop entrance, 'I'm going to get you closed down.'

Lazlo followed slowly. Maybe I could say something to calm him down? 'I have only shown you a small sample of the maps, sir.'

On exiting the shop, Provini threw the door back. Lazlo heard the sound of traffic outside and could feel cold fresh air enter his shop. As the door closed, the little bell rang out thrice.

Lazlo returned to his drafting table and his newest map, which had had plenty of time to dry. He unnecessarily blotted at it from north, south, east and west.

2. I AM NOT HERE

Pick and mix

I didn't do it. Whatever it is that you think I did. I wasn't there. I couldn't do that sort of thing – I'm not that type of guy.

Yes, OK, I am a guy. A man. A heterosexual – not that there's anything wrong with being homosexual – it's just … I'm not going to go there – it's a minefield … I am he/him – that's the modern identity parlance.

Someone called me a cis-male the other day. I told them: 'Don't tell me who I am!' I want freedom to do anything I want to do. Be anybody I want to be. 'Don't box me in!'

Being defined is a straight-jacket … Cis-male? I had to look it up online. Apparently, cis and trans are chemistry terms … Hand-on-heart, we're calling ourselves after different shaped molecules!

Titchy, smaller than an ant. Yes, I'd like to be the size of a molecule then no one would ask me questions about: Who I am? What I did? What I didn't do? What I could do? What I couldn't do?

It's nobody else's business so why do people stick their noses in? I wouldn't! I'm not that sort of person …

I've given too much away; you know too much.

I don't want to be seen. Being The Invisible Man: now that would be perfect.

Duck and dive

I've used the internet. I tried all sorts of different identities online. They call them profiles. Easy to change. You can write almost anything. Once you have your pseudonym, avatar or alias, you're off.

To name a few, I've been: Duckface; Eel; Free4Five; Gu££y.

I stopped when, in a chat room, I was told I was catfishing.

Yes, you can do all sorts of things online but I'm not good enough with computing. I don't even know how to get on the dark web.

I'm stuck in the real world.

Christmas cake

Trying not to deviate too much from the norm – that's the ticket!

When people look, I don't want them to notice me. I don't like the attention. I wear dull clothes: a leather jacket over my blue jeans and white T-shirt. Standing out would be terrible. But I don't 100% hide – that draws a different kind of attention.

Yesterday was sunny. I donned Ray-Ban Aviator shades –

cool but nearly as conforming now as blue jeans. An added bonus, they hide my eyes. But I don't want people to wonder why I'm wearing shades so I only feel comfortable on a sunny day, even if nowadays people have them on inside but then they're usually trying too hard to be cool. It's only standardised cool, so I don't mind that.

I went into Tesco's and picked up a basket. It felt so good strolling up and down the aisles. The people out to buy chicken, potatoes, peas, carrots, or whatever, were all wearing their conformity in blue, black, white and grey colours. Yes, we all want acceptance!

Filling the shelves there are the leading brands, like Colgate, Kellogg's and Heinz to be bought by those who want to be the same as everyone else. Then there are the generics, like an own-branded tin of tomatoes, to be bought by those who want an undistinguished product.

I was tempted by a Tesco Finest Rich Fruit Cake. We must follow the traditions at Christmas. But it was far too big for just one person.

I stuck into my basket my usual groceries, a squeezable bottle of black shoe polish and a family pack of monkey nuts. That made me hum: *Hey, hey, we're the Monkeys.* I'd forgotten milk so I went back to the ceiling-to-floor fridge and a woman in a pinny came up to me: 'Are you an undercover shop detective?' I looked around dramatically to ensure no one else heard me, lifted my shades to my forehead, looked her directly eye-to-eye and replied: 'Shh, don't tell anyone else.' Her eyes sparkled.

But, honestly, I was shaken by the approach so I went straight to the self-service tills, paid and left. My God, I've been giving off a store detective vibe without even knowing it!

There were crowds going toward my model housing estate. I like crowds. Being surrounded by a mass of people I'm safe. Being singled out is the first step to being noticed.

There are 667 flats in total in the seven non-descript blocks on the estate. The flats all look the same but are actually in three types either three-, two- or one-bed.

Back in my one-bedroom flat, I was trembling as I sorted my shopping. I made myself a cup of tea to calm down. I try so hard to be anonymous but in Tesco's I was made the centre of attention. That mustn't ever happen again! I needed to tweak my clothes. Add something to say I have a personality. I really fancied a nice slice of Christmas cake to go with my tea; I cursed not buying it earlier.

By today, I'd decided upon a hat – that indicates a personality, right. But of what type?

I, the chameleon, go out in my shades with my large carryall. There are many store detectives in Westfield – I know I'll blend in there. As I follow the flow of the masses into the shopping centre I worry about the CCTV cameras.

I go past a hairdresser: Salon Salvé. My hair is a bit of a mess but no one will notice once I'm wearing a hat. Yes, a hat will save me the expense, time and the scrutiny of sitting in a chair while a hairdresser stares at me.

I still haven't yet decided on which type of hat. Maybe I'm going too far out on a limb? Hats can equal flamboyance. It is going to have to be the most nondescript hat I can find.

After frequenting three shops, I discover the most basic available is a baseball cap. I take my shades off to try on a navy-blue one with a good shape, a six-panel crown. It fits well and I buy it. Outside the shop, I immediately pull off the price tag and put on my new piece of attire.

Knock, Knock …

Knock at the door

Who's there?

I was seen as undercover but not any more. I'm now partially in the public eye, rather than firmly at the fringes, walking through the mall with my shades and cap on. This is not the problem. No one is looking my way. But there is something I hadn't considered … Baseball caps are so American – the people who look at me see me as a Yank.

Gee, I try not to be at the center of things and I become all American without trying. God darn! Even my leather jacket is a bit like The Fonz's. I hum: *Monday, Tuesday … happy days!*

The Bull pub is ahead of me with its generic grey frontage. I enter to act out being a happy Yank. A tall man and a short woman are standing by the counter drinking cocktails. Initially, because they are wearing matching grey woollen coats, I assume they are a couple.

I lean on the counter. As I'm in dark glasses, when I order 'Soda!', I imagine I could be mistaken for a Hollywood star who's strayed into Shepherd's Bush.

'Coke?' asks the barman.

'No, soda … fizzy water.'

'Which type? Perrier?'

'No, from the soda gun will do.'

'Sure thing, Bro'.' Did the barman reply like that because I'm wearing this cap?

The woman of the couple says in an Estuary accent: 'He's one real bastard.' I (and perhaps the barman) would have said son of a bitch rather than bastard.

The man says: 'You've got to remain optimistic!' His accent reveals him as another Londoner, or perhaps from the south east of England. Whilst what he had said was excellent, as optimism is the American base of faith.

'Remind me to mention that bastard to the boss, will you?' Work colleagues! Two people of opposite gender rather than a couple. I have no idea if he is cis, trans, straight or gay. But I could tell from her flippant remark she was one amusement-oriented broad.

'Go girl, that's the way to get ahead!' The fella's response sounds like a basic US aspiration. I don't ever want to 'get ahead' – people are restricted by success and fame. It was the buffalo that roamed freely.

'I'll be the best!' she says. It's far too close to an American norm and that disturbs me. On receiving my soda water, I move towards the bar's shadows. I drink slowly until the couple of work colleagues leave.

I go back to the barman and say: 'How ya this fine day?'

'Can I get you anything else?'

'I'll have a Bud.'

'We have Bud Light on draught or bottles of Budvar or Budweiser?'

'A bottle of Budweiser, buddy.'

'Coming right up …'

I realise if the United Kingdom isn't working for me maybe I could request naturalisation from the US authorities. Before I apply on the relevant US government internet site, I'd need to get my background story right. I take my Bud and sit in a booth. From my carryall I take out a small pad of paper and a pen. This could be my lucky pen?

What would I write if I was composing a letter? *Dear Sir.* No, that's far too formal. *Hey Dudes, Please could you kindly send me the paperwork for becoming an American citizen. Make my day, Clint.* No, that's far too obvious. *Have a nice day, Yours, Brad.*

Brad's a good generic American name, isn't it? Yes, here's Brad with a Bud. Sounds good … This time next year I could be blending in with the New Yorkers in Central Park … or should I go Midwest, or Bible-belt, or California? Ah, the parts of the US are an even bigger minefield than the regions here in the UK!

I need a better way to disappear. Maybe I could take someone else's identity. If I pick someone who has died, everything I do can be hidden within the things they did. No, hold on, if it was someone without many friends or family who has disappeared (presumed dead) then very few people are going to know it's me. I take out my smartphone to search the web. I need someone who looks like me: Okay. Male. Mid 20s. Caucasian. Mousy brown hair. Boring name. Alan? Bingo!

I stuff my baseball cap into my carryall. I return to the main concourse of Westfield. The caterpillar must shed its skin in order to become a butterfly.

For a new identity I'd need a new haircut. I, Brad, arrive at Salon Salvé.

Man alive

As soon as he entered the Salon, Kimberly asks Brad all sorts of questions.

'No, I don't need my hair washed ... I did it this morning.'

Brad removes his leather jacket and puts his shades away.

Kimberly is a good-looking girl. 'Please take a seat.' She hangs the jacket on a coat-rack then disappears into a backroom.

From the fake-leather salon chair, Brad looks at himself in the mirror directly in front of him. Magazines are stacked on a shelf below the mirror. He opens the magazine at the top, *Hello*. On page 4, there is an article about liposuction. He turns the page: *At home with David Beckham*. It's Saturday today – lottery day. He'd buy £10 of tickets after his haircut. If he won big, he'd have everything David has: the beautiful wife, the millions in the bank, the flash watches, a fleet of sports cars and the great hair. Maybe he should ask Kimberly about hair transplants?

Kimberly returns and covers him in a gown of a black synthetic material. 'Doing anything nice this weekend?'

Why is she asking him that question? 'I don't know …'

'Saturday night is the best night, isn't it?'

Brad feels her hands in his hair. 'Yeah, OK I guess.'

'You'll look the part when I finish with you.'

'Great.' Brad wonders if she is attracted to him.

She sprays water on his hair before she starts combing, cutting and clipping. He likes the feeling of her body as it presses against his arm as she works. Perhaps he should have had his hair washed first, that way she'd have given him a relaxing head massage?

'I was at The Fridge last night. Do you know it, it's in Brixton? … It's a great club. Good music. Fit men.' Kimberly laughs.

He feels trapped. She seems to be pushing for him to say something personal about his social life. 'Usually, I just go down to the local with a couple of mates. They won't notice a new haircut. Blokes!'

'It is good to get all spruced up … you never know?'

What does she mean by that? Never know?

'You never know who you might bump into …'

'That's true enough.' He can feel her leaning softy against him again.

'It is like, we had the bass player from ABC in yesterday … well, that's what he said.'

Is she hinting something isn't quite right about what I've said? 'Who is ABC?'

'You know, '80s' music. Gold lame ... They did that golden oldie: *Who broke my heart? You did. You did ...*'

'He must be a pensioner by now.'

'He had highlights put in to hide the grey. He looks good for his age.'

She's definitely hinting that everyone is hiding stuff. 'The only '80s' record I know is: *Shows fear as he turns to hide. Aaah, we fade to grey.*'

'I don't think I know that one.'

'Visage ...'

'No, I don't think so.'

Twenty minutes later, Kimberly asks if he would like gel.

'Why not?' says Brad.

She runs gelled fingers through his hair. He looks at the mirror in front of him and grins: Better than a transplant.

Kimberly then steps away from him. He feels at a loss; he wants her to stand against him again. She picks up a handheld mirror and moves behind him to show him the reflection of the back of his own head. 'Don't you look nice.'

Ask for more

Tidy hair, ends in a straight line at his neck. He nods to himself: Hello Alan.

The reflection of a reflection seems to ripple; he's reminded of his own freckled boyish face mirrored in a pool of stagnant water.

Alan moves the back of his head from right to left. 'Yeah, that's great!' Should he ask for more?

Kimberly brushes hairs from his shoulders. Alan remains seated, deeply breathing, watching his nostrils widen and fall. She takes off his black gown then, using a broom, brushes his fallen hair into a small pile. With a dustpan, she disposes of all that remains of Brad into the trash can.

Lucky

I put on my leather jacket and delve into my carryall. If I'm lucky, I'll be able to part-exchange.

I take out two boxes. 'You're in luck … I can do you a portable bedside clock radio for £7 or two for a twelve, wonderful present?'

She shakes her head. 'It's £25 for the hair.'

'No, OK, never mind, here's …' I hand her two tens and a £5 note. 'See you.' I leave no tip.

I step out of the hairdressers and leave Westfield.

In the darkness, I'm invisible. I smell mince pies on the West London air. I saunter towards Shepherd's Bush market. A couple, in blue (his) and fawn (her) coats, walk beside me. She carries a large black and white cuddly owl. I like my invisibility.

There is a short gust of cold wind: 'Bloody hell!'

The man looks towards the source of the curse, at me. He has black hair that goes all the way to his collar. I grin inanely and stop walking to allow them to walk on alone. He saw me as danger. Me the outlaw!

My head is cold. Brad would have used the baseball cap. I could reach into my carryall and get it out now but a baseball cap is just not Alan.

I follow the couple at a distance. She is more interesting than him. Her black hair goes all the way down her back. She wears a tartan scarf and a fawn beret. The beret matches her coat. I can still just see the owl; its outline bobs in front of her.

They are holding hands. They are lovers. The owl must be a present for someone else's child. I don't think it's for their own child as their relationship seems too fresh. Perhaps this present is being used by each of them to confirm to the other that they like children.

And from the shadows, I stalk this love story.

Is love something I want too?

I've tried. The One didn't see me until I told her: 'I like you.' Then I'm a creep, when I could have been whatever she wanted me to be, if only she had told me what she'd wanted.

Why should others have what I can't have? Is love something I want to stop?

They cross the road then turn a corner. I follow stealthily. They take me down a road of family houses and stop in the front garden of one with a green door; the man rings the doorbell. I move to the shadows. The door opens. From my angle, I cannot see who is at the door. As the man disappears inside, the last thing I see is the woman offering up the owl.

I'm right! I don't usually like to crow at getting my guesses right but I am perceptive at being able to read people. No need for psychic powers.

I wait for a minute before moving forward to the front of the house. The number is clearly displayed on the gate: 41.

Time for fun.

Garden gate

I turn around and go to find a newsagent with a lotto poster in the window.

Inside, there is confectionary galore but I am not here for the sweets or chocolate.

I take out my lucky pen and select my numbers: Knock at the door – four. Man alive – five. Duck and dive – 25. Pick and mix – 26. Christmas cake – 38. I think of 41, but fun is not what I want. I want to: Ask for more – 34. The bonus ball is: 13.

I pay my money and buy a lottery ticket.

Yes, 13, unlucky for some, but surely lucky for Alan, Brad or another name? A win promises: a mind-blowing sum. I'll be rich. Everything becomes possible. I can be anyone ... I could be you.

3. MR DECUERVO

As I awaited my fate, I watched mother in the kitchen crouch down to pick up and put away a cotton tea towel. She didn't speak to me. I knew I was in trouble, I just didn't know yet what the punishment would be.

She wore a green silk dress cut off from her shoulders with a large skirt that could be ruffled up without losing its shape. This is the dress she usually wore at the dances. There were silver rings with deep blue stones on two fingers of her left hand. Her silver bracelet, with matching stones, dangled below her right wrist as she lifted the lid off a pot and poured cold water over oats. They would be left overnight to soak.

I could not tell if my mother was good looking but I knew she caught the eyes of many of the men in the village as they would ask her to dance. She only danced with father or Mr DeCuervo.

When she and my father danced, my sister and I giggled and treated it as a family game in which they were the core players and we were welcome participants. When she danced with Mr DeCuervo, we'd go and sit on the porch swing or lean on the windowsill and watch from a distance, not even looking at each other.

Mr DeCuervo liked to wear a blue suit. Father had commented: 'His suits fit him perfectly as they were tailored in Savile Row.' Mr DeCuervo always wore a pure white shirt with a matching smile, complemented with olive skin and straight back shoulders. With his thumbs in his trouser pockets and fingers splayed, he talked loudly to the other men about escaping our small and backward village.

Mrs DeCuervo occasionally came to our house but not recently. My sister Emily misses her visits as she used to braid her hair; her locks would become an abundance of corn rows and her cheeks somehow seemed less pronounced. Emily said it made her look beautiful.

Mrs DeCuervo faded. Emily and I had heard Mr DeCuervo say to her, before Sunday service: 'You could have made a little more of an effort.' Mrs DeCuervo burst out crying. I saw him whisper: 'Pull yourself together.' After the service, Mr DeCuervo thought he was alone with the priest when he explained: 'She feels she is dead inside. She told me: "I wish I was young again. Only the teenagers are alive." She bawled her eyes out.' The priest commented: 'It is no good if youth and looks are the things she values above everything else. Tell her to try to be more open to talk to God.'

Now, all Mrs DeCuervo seems to do is follow her husband around. She looks constantly tired, with shaded bags under her eyes on her triangular, floury face. It is like the sunshine has been withdrawn from her. In dark clothes, she has become a shadowy figure in the village.

To be honest, when she changed, I became scared of her and would pretend not to hear if she talked to me, not that she started many conversations. I felt bad that I ignored her, but she was bewitched by gloom, an infection I thought could be caught as easily as Spanish flu.

Mother moved to a cupboard and put away the rolled oats. She was finishing up. I didn't want her to catch my eye; I looked down to the black-and-white tiled floor. I knew I had done wrong. My punishment would come as soon as father returned. I might even be belted – though that had never happened before. What would it be?

*

A marquee goes up by our house at the start of summer. Every Saturday night, many of the families bring a blanket to spread out on the lawn to sit outside. Early in the evening they may eat foods like cold meats, cheese and bread. Invariably there would be somebody who had recently baked the local spongy biscuits for sharing.

Later people could just sit and chat, cool under the stars. Inside the marquee would be a different world, full of light and laughter. My father's friend, the farmer John Pettit, played guitar solo; or, to make up a three-piece band, the butcher and his wife joined him, with fiddle and flute respectively.

Then everyone was invited to join in on the dancefloor. Men

would pull from their pocket their dance cards, bearing a list of women's names, and seek out their first prospective partner. The atmosphere would be upbeat and carefree.

The only person who didn't like it was the priest; always on the periphery and not too popular. All night, he either stood in the doorway to the marquee staring at the dancers or patrolled the main road looking behind bushes or into ditches. If 'on duty' and he did find a hidden young couple he would give them a shoulder poke with his walking stick.

Father told me: 'For the priest, music is a distraction and too much beer is consumed. As both reduce inhibitions that leads to what he calls "The excesses". He only tolerates the Saturday nights because villagers go back to him for guidance, to follow God's laws, the next day.'

Everyone knew not to slow dance – otherwise the priest would shove his walking stick between the couple. The priest insisted: 'There has to be daylight between an unmarried man and a woman!'

If I was caught unaware, Mr DeCuervo would ruffle my hair and get me to carry his beer when he escorted mother on to the dancefloor. Emily kept her distance. When Mr DeCuervo talked to Emily, whatever he said, she would flush red in her cheeks.

Mr DeCuervo and mother only danced the fast dances like the jig or reel, and they danced as though they'd been waiting all their lives for each tune. My mother's movements got deeper and smoother, and Mr DeCuervo came alive, as though a spotlight had hit him.

She would return to father quickly, smiling and breathless, and, as if extra pleased to see him, touch him on the arm or around the waist. I would wonder, as he kissed her ear, what he whispered.

Mrs DeCuervo didn't dance with anyone, including her husband. My mother would make a point of going up to her and saying: 'You should dance, you are so pretty and a lovely dancer'. Mrs DeCuervo always replied the same way: 'Maybe next time'. There was no reason for her not to dance but two summers ago, like the turning of the leaves, she simply withdrew her card. She has not danced since.

This evening, summer almost over, inside the marque a few of the girls were dancing together. I watched John Pettit's daughter Clarissa, the most beautiful girl I had ever seen. She was dancing in a red gingham dress with a white waistband tied in a bow at the back. One, two, three, hop! One, two, three, hop! I suffered an unknown feeling whenever she focussed her attention on another lad. I wanted to whisper a dark threat in his ear.

Mother approached me and saw where I was looking. She asked me to accompany Mrs DeCuervo home at nine o'clock. I didn't want to go anywhere with Mrs DeCuervo; I wanted to walk Clarissa home. Instead of doing as I was told, I descended the stairs beside the covered shelter projecting at the back of our house, and hid in the basement. I felt bad as I waited twenty minutes in the darkness until Mrs DeCuervo went home alone. I'd also missed Clarissa going home.

*

Father, red faced, threatened me: 'We will meet again before the night is out!'

This led to Mother and Father arguing. Father's anger was clear to see in his ugly facial expressions. He shouted and thumped the kitchen table. I'd never seen anything like it before. He told Mother, 'Put Emily to bed. I'm going over to the DeCuervo's. I'll deal with him when I get back.' I knew I was to be punished, but what?

Mother asked: 'Where did this bad behaviour come from?'

I had no answer.

She told me to clean up in the kitchen.

I washed and dried dishes and two mixing bowls.

Once completed, she said: 'You need more structure and discipline. Now, sit and wait quietly for your Father.'

I didn't enjoy being forced to sit still and silent. My stomach and chest felt empty and hollow. Time was slow.

Mother set the breakfast table for the next day.

I'd disobeyed them: I couldn't breathe so I pinched at my knuckles. There are worse things than being belted; at least physical pain goes away.

What if they don't love each other any more? I understood how different Mother and Father are. I didn't like that they no longer shared a united front. I liked even less that Father had stormed off to the DeCuervo's.

I'm overwhelmed. Could my parents' divorce? Mother, Emily

and I end up living with the smooth Mr DeCuervo in some far-off city like London? I pray that I see Father again.

*

'You may feel I'm being a little harsh here.' Father twisted my right earlobe, his suitable punishment. 'Your mother and I love you son ... Why do you act in this way?'

I bowed my head. 'I don't know.' My left knuckle was red and raw.

'We bend over backwards to ensure that you have a good home. But I know you are now of an age I can't punish you into acceptable behaviour ... You should be old enough to know better than to disobey your mother and be incredibly rude to Mrs DeCuervo.' He tutted: 'So disrespectful to the DeCuervos ... Son, you need to treat people with respect.'

I repeated, 'I don't know.'

He talked about the ability for everything to change and how in spring when he sees the crocuses, he knows it is a fresh start for nature with warmer and brighter days to come.

I agreed with him on the need for a 'new start.'

4. ALBERT CLOCK

JUDICATURE (NORTHERN IRELAND) ACT 1978

THE CROWN COURT SITTING AT LANGSIDE

COURTHOUSE, BELFAST

IN THE MATTER OF THE CROWN

Complainant;

-and-

PRESTON JONES

Defendant.

TRN.005.004.7639

Thursday 8 April 2021

POLICE RECORDING TRANSCRIPT

BH: 09:35. Thursday 8th April 2021. Detective Sergeant Bobby Hamilton of the PSNI recording. I'm with the suspect. Please state your name, for the record.

PJ: Preston Jones.

BH: No middle name?

PJ: No.

BH: Date of birth.

PJ: 28th March 1979.

BH: And please state your address.

PJ: 188 Wesley Street, Lisburn BT27.

BH: Is that your permanent address? That was your parents' home.

PJ: Yes, I've been clearing out their things.

BH: You live in your parents' house?

PJ: Yes, it is my house now. They squirrelled away so much stuff. My dad used to say you never know if it's going to come in handy! I found old birthday cards I made back at primary school. It was sweet they kept them. I've had to throw so much away.

BH: Two days ago, Tuesday, we know you left Lisburn for Belfast.

PJ: Yes.

BH: The Lisburn train arrived at Lanyon Place station at 12:27pm. I want to hear the full truth in relation to the clock. Can you tell me what happened, in your own words, from the beginning?

PJ: As the train pulled into Lanyon Place, I heard the squeaking breaks and tasted metal in the air ... from the wheels against the rails.

BH: This is a serious matter!

PJ: Yes, I confessed —

BH: You are accused of violating a public monument! What you did was a fingers-up to Ulster, wasn't it?

PJ: No, I had to do it. I had no choice.

BH: Explain your version of events. You arrived at Lanyon Place. Take your time.

PJ: I descended on to the platform alone thinking, this was our real home? I had an hour and a half to kill, the appointment with the clock was at 2pm.

BH: The appointment?

PJ: I'll get to that … For all their lives, my mother and father ran a hardware store in Belfast City Centre. In better times, my dad joked: 'My only son was born on a bed made of 120 boxes of nails.' The store had our name 'Jones' above the door. The real owner was Lord Stokes Sr. When Lord Stokes Sr died, Lord Stokes Jr decided to cash in; he could see no need to own a hardware store in Belfast. He lives in Kent. To him Belfast is another country. My mum and dad were made redundant. Dad called it 'early retirement'. They moved to Lisburn but they never recovered. [Pause] Time is cruel. My mum and dad died four days apart from each other over Christmas. What more is there to say?

BH: Mr Jones? … For the tape, Mr Preston Jones has put his head in his hands. His body is shaking. He is crying … Mr Jones I will pause the recording for a moment, to give you a little time to compose yourself. It is 9:39.

*

BH: 09:57. Thursday 8th April 2021. Detective Sergeant Bobby Hamilton continuing the interview with the suspect. Please state your name?

PJ: Preston Jones.

BH: You were telling me you had an appointment with the clock. Was the date Tuesday 6th April of any significance?

PJ: No, not in particular ... I just had to wait until after Easter, ensure that my parents hadn't risen again.

BH: [Sigh] A crime has been committed. You seem to evade my questions, Mr Jones ... Let's get back to you getting off the train. What did you do after arriving in Belfast? Tell me slowly.

PJ: I walked towards Lanyon Place's exit. The light was bright as I walked past waiting taxis, up towards the High Street. It being lunchtime, the street was filled with office workers ... I needed a rest to put down my bag. I needed a smoke, Silk Cut. That purple and white packaging is another thing long gone. Everything changes, doesn't it? I lit up but never let go of the bag's strap, for the whole time that I smoked. I wondered if there was anywhere good for a bite to eat in St George's Market.

[Silence]

BH: Don't stop. [Cough] Go on ...

PJ: It looked like it was going to rain ... I settled on a cheese sandwich before the rain came down. I was annoyed with myself for not having a raincoat, umbrella or anything. I'm not the sort to be encumbered with wet-weather gear. Both hands free for the next smoke, so to speak. The rain developed into a heavy torrent. I had time to stop under an awning and waited.

BH: Get back to the point.

PJ: The way things keep on changing is the point. God is —

BH: Mr Jones, come on. Keep telling me what happened ... Give me the details.

PJ: Well, the rain stopped as quickly as it had started. It was as if God had poured a bucket of cold water over Belfast and then got bored and gone to play with some other part of the world. I knew I must get on to follow the path Jesus Christ had given to me.

BH: You have had your psychological assessment. You're not being detained under the Mental Health Order, Mr Jones. You've been arrested on a very serious charge. Please move forward with what actually happened.

PJ: I took a hi-vis jacket, with Belfast City Council written on the back, and a swipe card, with neck strap, from my bag and put them both on. I reached for a pen and a clipboard, before closing up the bag. [Pause] I made my way to Queen's Square and the sandstone clocktower ... I knew public access to the clock was barred but the tower had chosen me. It leans at an angle you see, like the tower in Pisa. The Albert Clock already told inclined time.

BH: The tower had chosen you? Okay, so, what was your plan at this stage, Mr Jones?

PJ: Plan?

BH: Or was there no plan and this was all done on a whim?

[Silence]

BH: You don't seem to understand the seriousness of your actions.

PJ: I let the carriage clock on the mantelpiece unwind. Dad had kept it wound. It was one of his regular chores. I think he liked to do it ... I stopped all their clocks at home. It wasn't enough.

BH: Is that relevant?

PJ: My plan was simple – to hide in blind sight … The base of the tower was cordoned off, as I knew it would be. The Council doing repairs – I guess it still is? The ground was wet as I passed the cordon easy enough. I remember the doorway and iron gate were open. I looked up at the life-sized statue of Albert as I entered … I went up the stairs. There were occasional slit windows that brought in a little light. I expected workmen further up, so I shouted: 'Malachy Franklin, are you up there?' I got no answer so I went upwards before repeating my question. This time, I got a reply, something like: 'There ain't no Malachy here. Who are you? What are yis up to?' I carried on up. I knew I'd reached my destination when I saw the working innards of the clock behind a red-faced man in a hi-vis jacket, just like mine. I wanted to reach out and touch the clock – touch time. I didn't. Instead, I spoke loudly: 'OK. Who are you?' I made ready with my pen hovering over the clipboard. He said: 'I'm Paddy … Paddy Smith. What's this all about?'

BH: We've interviewed Mr Patrick Smith and he says you made a fool of him.

PJ: No, I didn't … I told him: 'From the roster, it should be Malachy Franklin working here. There's been a number of incidents we don't want to see repeated.' He asked me who I was. I held up my fake swipe card, Mark Fitzpatrick.

[Silence]

BH: Go on …

PJ: Paddy was no fool. He said: 'I'm going to ring my supervisor.' I acted nonchalant and said something like: 'No problem with me, mate.' So, while Paddy phoned, I made a point of looking around. There was a black ladder up to the clock face. I could see cracks brought on by age in the face – a clock shouldn't age! Out of a little window, I saw the tops of trees swaying in the wind and the pavement bathed in daylight – as if everything in the world was fine.

[Sniff]

[Silence]

PJ: [Sniff]

BH: For the tape, Mr Jones is showing signs of distress again. His body is shaking ... Mr Jones, please continue with —

PJ: I'm sorry. [Sniff] I'm ... I'll be alright ... [Deep breath] So, when Paddy hung up, I simply asked: 'All sorted?' He said: 'Ach you know ... he'll get back to me.' So, I said: 'Oh, right ...' I left that hanging as if I didn't believe it and stared at him. A few seconds later, Paddy said: 'I really could ... you know ... the little boy's room.' I said, 'A man's gotta do what a man's gotta do.' I continued to stare at him. He said, 'Aye, can yer keep an eye on everything? It won't take long.' And, I said: 'Sure.' He left me on my own. I looked at my watch 1.55pm – result!

BH: To be clear, you were on your own with the Albert Clock?

PJ: Yes.

BH: Can you tell me why 1.55pm was a result.

PJ: My parents met for their first date by the clock at 2pm.

BH: So 2pm was special?

PJ: Yes. I took tools from my bag. I put my head up close to the cogs of a revolving wheel, I could see the problem. I reached into the mechanism and purposefully cut a wire; I left it dangling down the wall. The time, decorated by angels and gargoyles, was stopped. I needed it to stop.

The interview terminated at 11.06am on Thursday 8 April 2021.

5. ONE POUND AND ONE SHILLING

The front door of the house at 103 Cavendish Square was a royal-blue colour. Two mock-Greek pillars – one on each side – supported a triangular porch roof. Pep held a silver-topped cane in one hand and a linen bag in the other. He rapped on the door with his cane. His black top hat and black cloak were not out of place in this fashionable part of town. *I've been away too long.*

Pep removed his top hat and clasped it with the bag and cane all in his left hand. As he waited up on the doorstep, the gusting wind caught in his cloak showing red lining as it flapped. He turned his head to watch the hansom cab he had just exited pull away; the horses clattered into the distance.

He gazed southward; the view was grey buildings and a tower, upwardly spiking the horizon. He knew the city centre was the domain of beggars, thieves and street drinkers. The market at Billingsgate Wharf, with its expanded area for fish, would be open. The last time Pep had been there he had seen for himself the sheds in a state of decay, and drunks partying on a grass verge. *There are fish businesses closing down when all should be thriving!*

Pep turned back to the door as it slowly opened. He expected to see one of Farrell's servants. His heart stopped as he saw the pale figure in a silk dressing gown holding the door ajar. Pep raked the fingers of his free hand through his hair. 'I came as soon as I heard.'

'It's good to see you, Pep.' Farrell's response was slow and quiet.

Pep could make out a sour smell on Farrell's breath. He looked down at Farrell's red and swollen hands; the fingers looked too stiff to bend. 'I'm sorry, so, so sorry.'

'I missed you. I can't believe ... You look so ... you look great. What have you been doing?' Farrell leant on the doorframe.

'Oh, this and that ... I ... Dublin was good, the Guinness grand, as they say ... We explored the city. I like the architecture, very pretty in places, and friendly people.'

'Pep, why didn't you come straight back for the summer party? I —'

'It didn't feel right to celebrate and, you know, they are for your fellow members and colleagues ... I visited a doctor in northern Dublin, I needed to find out ...'

'You ... You didn't ...'

'It was busy, very hectic. You know I need to press on in business. I took a look at what they have done at their Smithfield marketplace; very interesting.' There was a clunking sound as a bicycle pushed by on the road. Pep continued: 'But I'm here now for as long as ... I've brought you a barmbrack and soda bread.'

Farrell opened the door wide. 'Please put it on the sideboard, will you? I'm going to need more than .... I'm going to lie down now.'

Pep scraped his handmade shoes on the bristled door mat. 'Where are your servants?'

'I've let them go. I can fend for myself.'

Pep carried and hung his black hat and cloak from a peg attached to the wall beside the front door. He walked straight to the kitchen. There was a slightly medicinal smell from a topical ointment and one of the wall kitchen lamps was leaning to the left. Pep put the provisions down on the sideboard as he had been asked, and adjusted the unlit lamp to its correct vertical position.

Pep joined his friend in the parlour. The room had more clutter than Pep remembered. Beneath an odour of furniture polish, he could detect a faint tinge of jasmine, both scents countering the smell of decay. He stood on the luxury (mainly red) Egyptian rug, the window to his right. The furniture looked unchanged. The two dark wood cabinets full of books were still on the left. Many with Farrell's name written in gold on the spine. None of the books touched. Farrell used to be always working to try to better model biology, now he lay on a blue chaise longue in the light. The dressing gown had risen up one arm, it was the first time Pep had seen Farrell's veins sticking out so prominently.

Pep stuttered: 'I ... I ... can't look at you like this. You will get better surely.'

'I don't think so.'

Pep turned away, as if to leave, but didn't. 'I was never any good for you – not good enough. You always knew that, Farrell. You of all people, a scientist!'

Farrell scratched his leg through his gown.

'My life,' Pep said, 'made me who I am. A snake will bite however much you love it. I was never a faithful man.'

Farrell still didn't reply. Pep changed the subject: 'I've been asked to invest in a purpose-built fish market on Lower Thames Street.'

'What are you going to do?'

'I'm in. The population of London is growing. Fish is a staple. It's a certainty.'

'I'm pleased for you.' There was no enthusiasm in Farrell's voice.

Pep looked down at his handmade shoes on the rug. 'How are you sleeping?'

'I try to practise good habits but it is difficult. The pain is worse at night.'

Pep caught an intertwined smell of Farrell's stale sweat and jasmine. 'I've heard of a refuge known for growing plants that serve a medicinal purpose. They have an apothecary garden with plants from all over the world ... You always used to stress the "potent power in the naturally active ingredients in botanicals".'

'Can I have a glass of water?' asked Farrell.

'Yes, of course.'

Pep went back to the kitchen. He took a clean glass and turned on a tap. He let it pour for five seconds. Seeing Farrell was more difficult than he had expected. As he waited, he took deep breaths. He needed a breather.

When he put the glass under the cold running water, he saw his hand was shaking. Once the glass was full, he turned the tap off and poured the water in the glass away. He rubbed the glass slowly with a tea towel before putting the glass and towel down. He pinched the top of his nose and closed his eyes. *Can I do this? Can I really help?* Regaining composure, he opened cupboards for a tray, jug and second glass. He filled the jug with cold water, put it and the two glasses on the tray and returned to the parlour.

Pep poured water from the jug into one of the glasses, then handed it to his friend. Farrell sipped at the water. Pep stood beside the chaise longue, feeling awkward. 'We could take sanctuary at this refuge.'

'I'm not going anywhere.'

'Didn't you once say that by using plant-derived compounds we could synthesise the drugs to cure —'

'Please don't …'

'The use of plant extracts was something you used to believe in.'

'I don't want false hope anymore.'

Farrell's words felt like yet another dream lost. Pep sat down on the edge of the chaise longue, his back to Farrell. They sat in silence. A memory was triggered for Pep: Twenty years earlier, a time of great hope.

Farrell returned from a library visit and deposited books on the parlour floor. I had been waiting and told him to hurry up and get ready. 'We don't want to be late.' He was young, virile and every bit the great scientist then.

I watched him dress in his best finery: on went a bright white cotton shirt, that I could smell was recently starched. Gold cufflinks, I had bought him, went on at the wrist. He asked for my advice, 'Which is the best-quality suit?' I suggested the new one 'where the trouser leg is narrow at the ankle.' A double-breasted waistcoat of a design that echoed his jacket was also chosen. Farrell's waistband remained just visible below the waistcoat. I picked out a blue tie that matched his eyes. He laced up his round-toed black Oxfords, then put on his frock coat that narrowed his waist and seemed to pull back his shoulders. To finish, he collected his black gloves and a tall, cylindrical top hat. I suggested one last thing, wrapping a silk cravat around his neck.

Farrell gathered up his lecture notes into a single pile and placed them into a folder. We ventured to the Royal Society by hansom cab.

As I sat at the back of the lecture theatre, Farrell presented his findings to his peers with all the vocabulary of his field. 'Many people used to think nature and biological phenomena could never be understood by humans. Mathematical models have helped biologists understand molecular interactions. As we move to greater understanding, we start to decode life systems. Through mathematics we see basic principle in nature. We have created theory after seeing pattern in cell biology. Now, we can model cell biology.' He went on to talk of 'differential equations' used to 'model a non-linear system'. He scrawled exotic symbols (to me) onto a blackboard.

He'd practised his lecture on me so I knew he's near the end when he says: 'Insights made from modelling can be carefully evaluated when compared to

43

findings from experimentation in living systems.' He finishes to much applause. I felt so proud of him.

We left via the corridor of presidents' portraits; the stern old men looked like they had filled those walls forever.

Black came up and seized Farrell by the hand and shook it vigorously: 'That was amazing! I've spent too long looking through a microscope, I'd forgotten how exciting modelling nature can be!'

'It gives us hope.'

That's when Black suggested a drink to celebrate.

'The Guinea is close,' said Farrell.

In the cab, Black and Farrell discussed some detail of his study of cell growth. We got to Bruton Place as sacks of grain were being hoisted to a loft next door to the pub.

Inside, we sat on wooden benches, wooden screens giving a sense of privacy from other customers. The atmosphere was cosy. The Guinea is one of the few genuinely timeless pubs.

'Guinea fowls are normally monogamous creatures, mating for life,' said Black.

Farrell laughed. 'You do know this pub is named after the coin!'

'Of course, I do! I was passing comment on you two.'

'I've been called "shilling" for telling people I'm going to make my fortune and I don't care how I do it.'

'And, Farrell is the pound?' asked Black.

Farrell laughed again – he was obviously relieved his lecture was over.

We ate steak pie, I think Black had the steak and kidney, and we drank pints of Young's bitter.

'Farrell, we are on the brink of scientific revelation!' stated Black.

'Yes, we are finding truths in nature that will —'

'No more religious mumbo-jumbo!' bellowed Black.

'Do you really think that can ever be left behind?' asked Farrell.

'It's being left behind now, Farrell. It already is —'

'Ha! I'll drink to that,' said Farrell.

Farrell and Black were so buoyed by ambition; it made me happy; it was a time of joy. As the night wore on, the Guinea became full of frivolity. We stayed late.

Pep had been looking towards Farrell's book cabinets but not seeing them. The good feeling from remembering the simpler time was fading. He said: 'Do you remember when you and I and Black were at the Royal Society together and went drinking in the Guinea?'

Farrell shrugged.

Nothing is as it was! Pep knew Black was dead of course, the last time Pep had been to the Royal Society and Guinea, the Royal Society superficially remained the same while the Guinea was closed for repairs as the roof supports had suffered from damp. 'Your faith in science used to be fundamental to you.'

'Yes, I used to think my work mattered.' Farrell shifted forward and back on the chaise longue as if looking for a more comfortable position. 'I felt fortunate to be able to add to the body of knowledge but —'

Pep stood up to look at his friend. 'You used to say it was for something greater.'

'Hope is of little … Now, it doesn't matter.'

'Farrell, you will always be remembered for making a difference.'

Farrell looked back at Pep blankly. 'What does any of it really mean?'

Pep moved uncomfortably on his spot of rug. 'Oh Farrell …'

'Nothing matters, Pep. We all turn to dust.'

'Ashes to ashes is priest talk. You're not dead yet … I'm sorry. Over the years, I have learnt so much from you, Farrell … I truly admire you.'

'Thanks.' A little red developed in Farrell's cheeks.

Pep looked towards Farrell's desk; the awards on the wall and books on the desktop, had not changed since Pep had last been in Cavendish Square.

In the few seconds Farrell didn't speak his cheeks paled. 'A part of me dies whenever I'm with … or when we are apart, Pep.'

Farrell looked like he wanted to speak again but he fell back on the chaise longue and was silent. Pep did not know what to say. Beside the desk, blankets and embroidered cushions were piled on top of a couch he remembered when Farrell had worked late; he often read and fell asleep using those very blankets and cushions.

Pep knelt down beside Farrell and held his hand. Pep knew he wouldn't be able to say what he wanted to say if he looked at his friend directly so he bowed his head. 'I wasn't able to be close to anyone. I thought it would just be more pain whenever that relationship was taken away. I didn't realise how foolish …' Pep lifted his head, to face Farrell, 'I will stay with you for as long as it takes – it was *you* that taught me to be honest first and foremost.'

'Oh Pep, I don't want you to be here out of guilt. I never —'

'It's not guilt ... I left because of what was going on in my head. I return because I want to be with you.' Pep felt uncomfortable.

Farrell tried to look directly into his eyes. 'Are you really being true to yourself?'

'Of course ...'

'You called yourself a snake a few minutes ago.' Farrell held very still in his seated position. 'Aren't you still that snake?'

Pep made eye-to-eye contact. 'You misunderstand —'

'Do I?'

'I, like the snake, do what I want. And what I want to do is be here with you.'

'Your snake eyes can be mesmerising.' Farrell's brow puckered as he smiled.

'I want to be with you,' said Pep.

Farrell didn't speak.

'Didn't you hear me? All I want to do is be here with you.'

'I'm not looking for anyone's pity,' said Farrell.

'For as long as ... forever.'

6. KILL VERONICA POUND!

I awoke with a weight of sadness – that was the first thing I recognised. Then came a bad stench.

On opening my eyes, I saw I lay on a tilted backwards chair with leg stirrups and the walls around me covered in light and dark-blue tiles going up about 12 foot.

I looked upwards at a huge white operating theatre light hanging down from the ceiling, directly above, like a mock sun. The ceiling was marked where paint had peeled off.

I felt extremely itchy in and around my groin and bum. All I had on was a pair of ragged knickers. The stench came from me – I felt disgust. How could I have soiled myself?

One side of my threadbare knickers was completely ripped, the other frayed. As I took them off, they fell apart. My hands were dirty; my nails jagged, old nail polish had risen from the cuticle. How long had I been out? I threw the knickers into a corner of the room, where an old window frame and cupboard doors leant up against the wall. I scratched at sores on my inner thighs – until my skin was red and raw. It did not soothe my sores.

I wanted a shower – good and hot.

I clambered off green plastic cushioning that covered metal and stood up. My bare feet felt something sharp underneath crumble to powder; it had been a white strip of fallen paint, lying with many others strewn across the floor. I brushed away dried paint that had got caught between my toes.

I examined where I had sat. It was an operating chair and the leg stirrups hung off the end like lost arms. There was a large rectangular grey metal box on the floor, from which a cylindrical piece of metal held up the adjustable chair. Why had I been lying there? Had someone done something for me … to me?

I scanned the room: a broken-off headrest lay five foot away. A built-in cupboard had large square holes in it and the wood was splintered where hinges had been. A metal door marked 'Exit'.

I rushed to the door and pushed my way into a green corridor. Blue strips – at two-inch and waist height – protected the walls. Things must have regularly been moved around in this corridor. Discarded used masks littered the floor. I ran barefoot over laminate, towards a set of double-doors with frosted glass panes. The temperature dropped and I breathed in fresher air. Ahead I could see, beyond glass, natural light. I fled through a large rotating door into a street.

The sunlight was that of a subdued early afternoon. I was acutely aware of the air on my skin. I needed to get some clothes on before someone saw me.

A few paces forward, I realised that something was wrong

with the surroundings: it was absolutely silent. I saw an office block, abandoned cars and a shopping trolley. No cars in motion and nobody about. Around the office block, I should have been seeing workers. Everything was manmade yet there were no men, except an eight-foot face of a Coke Zero Man bringing a giant can to his lips.

I asked myself: *Why am I not seeing anyone alive? What's really weird is there's no body dead either. Has all organic material been vapourised?*

A road sign read Midway Park Road. Across the road, an underground station; another sign: Midway Park – I didn't recognise the name. An empty telephone box sat adjacent to the station.

Gravel bit into my left foot as I crossed the road. Might there be somebody at the station? A grille across the entrance confirmed what I'd already guessed – the station was closed. The windows were all locked too. I shook the grille and shouted 'Hello!'

What next? The telephone box. I put the phone to my ear – no dialling tone.

There was no one at Midway Park. Where was everyone! Was everywhere going to be like Midway Park? Were there people elsewhere or was I the only one left on the planet?

Feeling itchy, I scratched myself again. I needed answers; I also needed clothes and the building where I had woken up seemed like the best place to find them both.

I crossed back over the road and noticed for the first time a Midway Park Hospital sign. And that was when I saw it. I screamed. Letting out the noise felt good.

I made my way towards the human shape hanging in mid-air.

Tied to the curved part of a lamppost, a body, held by the throat, hung from a rope.

I felt the urge to cough as I moved closer to a life-sized rag doll with black buttons for eyes. In its fake hands it held a sign commanding 'Kill Veronica Pound!' As if to emphasise the point the two 'O's had been crossed out.

I looked at the head. Do I see a grimace on its face? Is that rag doll meant to be me? Am I Veronica Pound? Why would someone do this?

I really didn't like the stuffed effigy dangling mid-air. I wanted to take it down but there was no way for me to get up the lamppost. The effigy would remain strung up, hanging by a noose. Why black button eyes when my eyes are blue?

A memory from when I was 15 came to me. My mother said something about 'her betrayal'; why?

Mother had told me: 'You're acting strange, probably the Tartrazine in the orange drinks we give you.' Father called my misbehaviour 'teenage rebellion' – he was hosting a dinner party to impress his boss that night.

My mother was bringing in the dessert when I appeared naked before them. Mother had tears in her eyes when she wrapped me in her black velvet jacket. She tried to hold my hand in hers – I pulled mine away. I fought as father tried to placate his guests. I knew I needed to be natural in an unnatural world.

In the silence of Midway, I recognised my nakedness now as a manifestation of that 'being natural'.

Mother escorted me back to my bedroom. She held me wrapped in that velvet jacket, and said: 'I've rung for help as I want to protect you.' Maybe half an hour later, the doorbell rang and mother took me downstairs. The stranger who called himself doctor shone a light into my eyes and asked me questions, then offered me three little white pills, which I rejected. I didn't know the man; for all I knew, he could have been trying to kill me. I started shouting: 'We all need to be free!' The guests had left by then but my father was angry: 'I'll be a laughing stock on Monday.' He paced the room: 'For God's sake Honey, take the bloody pills!' Mother told me: 'It's all right, they are perfectly harmless.' I refused to take the pills. After a couple of hours, more men arrived. One of the strangers talked to my parents about my safety, never once speaking to me, and my parents gave their permission. When he loaded a syringe with God knows what, I hit out. As the man injected me, three others and my mother held me down. Where was father? *I shouted at my mother: 'Judas!' I was taken to a car, my mother crying as she walked alongside. I blacked out.*

Yes, when love is withdrawn, you have a choice: Do you go down? Or do you fight?

That first time: *I heard a loud noise, like a bomb, and saw in my mind a ball of yellow light rise up into a grey sky. The sky coloured red and yellow, as if on fire. The ground cracked open. But I held back the nightmare. I came around in a hospital, breathing hard and sweating.* That time I awoke I was wearing clothes. The psychiatrists told me: 'With medication and restraints we can make you better.' The pills made me sick. The restraints made me angry.

My parents didn't even pretend to love me after that. How can you love something that you are scared of? *My mother apologised: 'I lied, forgive me ... I should not have lied. And I should not have passed you over to someone else's care. I did what I thought was best for you but now I feel ... I'm your mother, I should have been able to provide you with whatever you need.'*

So, it had happened again. I can remember my parents, why can't I remember my name, just Honey.

A gust of wind put movement into the effigy. It swung back and forth slightly. I felt around my neck, imagining the tie. I am Veronica Pound! Was my entire weight to be suspended by a rope noose, stretching my neck to breaking point? The people of Midway wanted me, vertically, dangling from a lamppost?

'Oh god, please no!' I cried.

They shouldn't have brought me here to the Midway Hospital. Did I not hold back in my retaliation?

Could this be my doing? Did energy turn skin, hair, flesh and bone to dust? There should be some memory from people-destroying rage. But I don't remember anything.

I returned to the hospital. The phones didn't work but I did find clothes and a ladder. I was able to cut the effigy down.

I'll follow the road signs to the nearest town, just five miles away. I need to check for life. Maybe there'll be a phone that works there and I'll be able to call my parents.

If alive, whatever they said last time, I know my mother would come for me.

7. TRANSMISSION

On picking up my phone, I heard: 'It's Bianca …'

'Oh, it's been —'

'Jeff, I think you need to get yourself checked out. I've tested positive for chlamydia.'

'OK.'

'That's what comes of having unprotected sex,' Bianca told me.

Is she's telling me off for giving it to her? 'You said it would be fine without protection …' As soon as I had started, I knew apportioning blame was a mistake.

'It certainly wasn't me who decided not to use a condom!' said Bianca.

'I didn't mean —'

'Jeff, I'm not accusing anyone of anything. I was seeing Frank and I'm still seeing Georgie, off and on … I'm ringing around … all my sexual partners.'

'So, you're ringing … you could have given it to me?'

'Yes, exactly, that's why. Deciding not to use a condom doesn't even sound like me, I can't fully remember, to tell the truth. You told me you were a serial monogamist, Jeff … we were both pissed, weren't we? And it was a while back.'

'How long ago would I have to go back if I have it?' *I'll have to call Sarah, then there's Linda. I've been seeing Maria …* 'Jesus!'

'Don't panic. Go to a clinic. Check yourself out. You might be fine … If not, do what I'm doing. It's OK, like a personal test and trace. It's better to tell people in person rather than contact tracers.'

*

I spent Friday morning worrying. *Have I got it? I was so stupid.* The internet informed me the local hospital had a walk-in clinic.

Making my way there, I saw a big sign inside the bus: 'Wear a face covering at all times. A mask clearly impedes the spray of droplets from the wearer – it also gives some protection to the people near you.' Everyone was compliant downstairs.

The seated passengers, including me, sat one person for every two seats. The message on social distancing is to avoid contact or stay more than two metres away from other people.

As the bus filled up, I felt increasingly twitchy. I had so many unanswered questions: *Who transmitted? Who received?* I imagined a different outcome: *Bianca could have rung me to tell me she was having my baby! Blimey!*

The bus driver left people standing at the bus stop when the bus had 30 passengers upstairs and down – it was at about half normal capacity. It was only a couple more stops to the hospital.

On exiting the bus, I pulled my light-blue paper mask down to my neck, to get a little fresh air on the short walk to the hospital front entrance. I put my mask back on before entry.

I bought an *i*-newspaper at the newsagent in the main foyer, then followed the blue and white signs towards Sexual Health. *Maybe I haven't got it? I should have worn a condom!*

The hospital corridors were full of masked people, both medics and patients, looking busy. *Are people going to the same place as me? I wonder if I'll recognise anyone I know at the clinic? Oh God, what are they going to want me to do? It's bound to be embarrassing.*

At the sexual health clinic reception, two masked women sat behind a Perspex screen in their own sealed-off little area. In front of them, squatting on the counter, a large hand-gel dispenser carried a prominently displayed sign: 'For customer use.'

To the left of the reception was a waiting area; two couples and two single men were seated. *No one I recognise. No one I'd consider having sex with.* To the right of the reception was a table and then three doors: Consulting Room 1. Consulting Room 2. An unmarked grey door.

I went up to the prettier receptionist. She had tied-up wavy hair and was wearing a baggy Arran jumper. I whispered: 'I'd like a chlamydia test. An old girlfriend told me to — '

'We can do the test here. But we will need to inform your GP unless you want to keep your identity confidential?' She gave me a cursory glance.

'No, that's fine.'

She pushed a form and a biro through the double letterbox-sized gap at the bottom of the screen. Her hands were concealed by light-blue latex gloves. 'Please can you fill this out.'

I took the form and pen to the waiting area and sat down. One of the couples are gossiping about someone called John who became so ill he had to go on a ventilator. Everyone else was silent. I avoided catching anyone's eye. I was embarrassed enough already. *I'm glad I'm wearing a mask.* I concentrated on filling out the form.

Once done, I returned everything to the receptionist. She looked over my paperwork, cleaned the biro with a wet wipe and gave me a raffle ticket-sized piece of paper with a code on it: TZC-1746. 'Would you like to see a male or female nurse? It might take a little longer, if it matters.'

'No, I don't mind.'

'Please wait and the nurse will call out your number.'

'Thanks.' I sat down in the waiting area, there were now four single men (including me) but just one couple (the friends of John). I hadn't paid enough attention to know whether John had survived (or not).

I tried to not look at any of them but I couldn't stop myself. I definitely did not want to be spotted looking out of the side of my eye at the comings and goings. Catching someone's eye would be too embarrassing.

They all looked away from each other too. *Everyone's anxious.* I got out my newspaper more for cover than because I wanted to read.

About ten minutes later, a masked Asian-looking man in his

late 30s, in a white lab coat and blue latex gloves appeared from somewhere and called out: 'T Z C 1 7 4 6.'

I put my newspaper away in my pocket and followed the nurse into Consulting Room 2.

He sat down at his desk. I sat two metres away. On the top of his desk were papers, a few pens, a wrapped Tesco's prawn mayonnaise sandwich, a computer and printer.

He asked me about my sexual history. I told him about the last few months and that at least once the sex had been unprotected. I wanted to ask for reassurance that I wasn't a complete idiot: a condom isn't a 100% guarantee of protection, is it? I heard the answer in my head: it would have given some protection!

Turning my eyes upward, above his head was a shelf of sexual health books: *The A-Z of Sex and Reproduction*. *Good Vagina Health*. *Pleasure and Rights* by Dr T. *The Psychology of the Penis*. *The Contraception Handbook*.

'Why do you think you have chlamydia?' he asked.

'Bianca, my ex-, rang me as she had been tested positive.'

'Do you have any of the symptoms?'

'I don't actually know what the symptoms are. I haven't noticed anything different, yet.'

'OK. If you have chlamydia it may be asymptomatic. But some of the things to look out for are: an unusual discharge from the end of your penis; an itching or burning sensation in the tube that carries the urine out of your penis; or any unusual pain when urinating or in your testicles. OK?'

'I've not had any of those, thank God,'

He handed me a leaflet titled Chlamydia Fact Sheet and said: 'Chlamydia is a fairly common STD. It is very good that you came in – it can cause infertility in women. Best to get it sorted out, if there is anything there. It can be quite easily treated.' The nurse then added, in what I felt was a condescending voice: 'Can you abstain from sex until you get your result?'

'How long will it take before the result?' I fold and pocket the leaflet.

'A week. Maybe 10 days.'

'Yes, of course, I can abstain for 10 days.'

'A couple of final questions. Have you urinated at all in the last hour?'

'No.'

'Have you taken any antibiotics in the last 24 hours?'

'No.'

'Good.'

He printed out and attached a sticky label with the code TZC-1746 on to a small transparent plastic sample bottle with cap.

He passed the small bottle with a pre-printed sheet of paper and a cleaning pad to me. 'Please follow the instructions provided. You will need to urinate into the container I've labelled, at least half the way up.' Immediately I was stressed about the procedure and the potential embarrassment if I got anything wrong.

The nurse took me back out to the reception.

'Please place your sample in the tray over there.' He pointed to a green plastic tray marked 'Sample' on the table.

'OK.'

'There's a cubicle through that door.' He pointed towards the unmarked grey door on the left.

'Thanks.' I walked through the grey door. The cubicle contained a toilet, sink and mirror.

I read the instructions. The steps to follow were carefully set out.

I gave myself a long hard look in the mirror. The light-blue mask over my nose and mouth hid my face and this, together with my average-length, thinning mousy hair, meant I could be almost anyone. The end of my *i*-newspaper stuck out of the pocket of my navy-blue anorak. *I'm pleased I look so non-descript. Even if one of the other people in the clinic were an acquaintance, they'd not be sure it was me.*

Before urinating, I washed my hands. I cleaned the head of my penis with the cleansing pad. *The Covid test is so much easier – just sticking something up your nose at home.*

I opened the small bottle. *I'm going to screw this up – trying to pee into the tiny bottle.* I started to pee into the toilet, then moved the open bottle under my stream. *It's fine.* I collected urine up to and over the mark, half the way up. I finished urinating back in the toilet. I put the lid back on. *And there's none on my hand either.*

Even though they had remained clean, I washed my hands again.

Coming from the toilet, I held the small bottle in one hand. It was warm, which seemed odd even though it was obviously not. *Body temperature.*

A large man, wearing a white lab coat, was complaining to the receptionist I hadn't talked to. He was telling her off, as he had been waiting far too long for something. I went back to the pretty receptionist: 'All done!'

She didn't look up. 'Please place your sample in the sample tray ... You should hear back from us with your result in between seven to fourteen days.'

I did as I was told, then returned to the counter. I held a hand under the nozzle of a hand gel dispenser and pressed the top. I rubbed my hands slowly with the alcohol gel.

It'll be such a relief if I don't have to ring around.

*

After a little fresh air outside the hospital, I pulled my mask over my nose and mouth before getting on the bus to go home. I could smell the sickly/sweet odour of my own stale breath. *I need a new mask.*

On the bus, I sat downstairs again. There was the same bold sign: 'Wear a face covering at all times.' *I'll definitely wear a condom at all times from now on!*

After a few stops, there were three people on the bus with face coverings, including myself, and three (a couple and a man) without. The man, in jeans and a tight jumper, had got on without any face covering. The woman with him had pulled her red and yellow scarf down, away from her mouth, as soon as she had passed the driver. The solitary man, wearing tinted green glasses and a white shirt with Urban Hype written across the front, had a paper mask dangling around his neck, as if he was too cool to wear it correctly.

I commented on the situation, projecting my voice: 'What is the point of having a sign saying "Wear a face covering at all times" if people just ignore it?'

My question particularly irritated the man from the couple: 'Mind your own business.'

As the bus stopped at a traffic light, I got up and walked to the front to stand beside the glass screen shielding the driver. I repeated my question: 'What is the point of having a sign saying "Wear a face covering at all times" if people are just going to ignore it?'

The driver, in both protective mask and gloves, grunted. I didn't know if it was in the positive or negative.

I continued: 'These rules must be difficult for drivers – there are going to be more irate passengers. You must be told not to get involved.'

He grunted again, this time he also nodded to show agreement.

The lights changed to green so I went to sit down again. On passing, the man from the couple said: 'Get out of my space. You're not two metres away from me.'

'You're not wearing a mask.'

'That's my choice. Get out of my space!'

'I am two metres away … The sign beside you says "wear a mask" but you don't wear a mask. I —'

'Fucking —'

'I asked what was the point of the sign?'

'Fuck off!'

I moved and sat down on the seat directly behind the solitary man. The atmosphere was tense for several stops: Nobody spoke. Nobody looked at each other. It reminded me of the waiting room at the clinic.

The couple prepared to get off the bus. When they disembarked, the man pulled a light blue mask from his pocket and waved it at me. He shouted: 'I'm a free man!'

I watched their backs as they walked away. I was amused. The man had proclaimed 'I'm free' whilst proving he was not, by always carrying the mask he so obviously despised.

Then I remembered I always carry a condom in my wallet, including on that night.

8. LETTERS FOR MONIQUE

Alastair Smithson

Peabrook Group

Chancery Lane

London WC2A

July 2009

Dear Monique,

I shouldn't be writing to you after so long: four years! But I still don't like it how we left it in the garden centre. I can't help myself – I <u>still</u> can't help myself. What do I want? I hear you ask. I think about you and want you. What a way to start a letter!

What can I say? I'm here for you if you wanted me for something. No, that's not enough. I love you. That's still true but it is too much I know. And, but – there is always a 'but' – there is another.

Denise and I are to be married. I think you would approve of her – I'd like that. She keeps my feet on the ground. Not like you!

64

Denise was a trainee when I first met her. It was at an all-staff function. I was introducing the new Chief Executive and she was standing to the side on her own holding a plastic cup. She wore a short black dress, I noticed her tanned legs (you know how I have always had a thing about fine legs) so I went over and said 'hello'. Work talk seemed to impress her – I suggested we go for a pizza afterwards. Pizza Express. It was very friendly. I don't know why I did it, we didn't have that much in common, but it felt obvious and physical. My body needed comfort.

I know you told me, the last time we talked, that we shouldn't meet up. But it doesn't stop me wanting you. We shared everything, you and I. What I want to do, at the very least, is continue not to have any secrets from you. But then that means I have to admit I still want you carnally. That's too vulgar. In my head, I want to have my cake and eat it too! Funny really, I think you would be able to keep something like that a secret – but I couldn't cope. It wouldn't be an enjoyable affair for me. I'd feel torn and guilty cheating on Denise.

So, Denise and I are to be married and I will not be contacting you again. But what I need to say is, that … it doesn't stop me wanting and loving you.

Ali xxx

Alastair Smithson's Diary

March 2005

Monique wouldn't talk to me when I phoned. Then she said: 'Yeah, hi, I'm busy right now. I'll call you.' She never did.

I wrote her a short note asking to meet up, posted it first class but got no reply. I knew I needed to go around to the garden centre, where she worked.

I waited outside the front entrance for an hour that Thursday. Overhead, the sky overcast, migratory birds escaped through the clouds.

I went in when I couldn't wait any longer. The plant saplings in red plastic pots and the mock Gothic furniture were nice – it didn't look cheap – so what if it was fabricated. I remembered our garden; it was all earth and twigs, and moist fungus that glistened. The worst, the very worst, we found whilst exploring amongst small bushes of fern, at the bottom, up on the cold shadow-side of the trunk of the oldest-tree, fungus that looked like a fried egg.

The bird baths, garden swings, mini houses and ponds all blended with my view of what is right for a modern garden. The fashionable water feature is just an update on the traditional multi-coloured gnome, sitting on a toadstool, fishing. Water reminded me of that rowing boat in Regent's Park, when the sunshine poured down on us. Monique was in a fluffy white dress, golden bangles and a scarf. I should have made more of that opportunity, that missed opportunity, to rekindle ... Why hadn't I at least tried again to touch the ultimate?

I approached a woman at the till. 'Where do I find Monique?' She stared at my face the way people do when they don't know you but see some resemblance of someone else. I was directed to a little office at the back.

As soon as Monique saw me, she asked 'Why didn't you call first? You can't just turn up like this.'

'Why are you ignoring me?'

She looked away ashen faced. 'We can't talk here.'

It wasn't that long ago we would have embraced on meeting, now there was embarrassment.

She stood up from her desk and walked out into the garden centre. I followed. I asked: 'How have you been keeping?' She stopped and turned to face me. She was pleasant but I could tell she really wanted to get away.

I wanted to rekindle what little we had had. I put a hand on her shoulder. It was only a tiny movement but Monique flinched. 'I don't think we should meet,' she said.

All I could do was splutter.

She simply walked away. I was left standing by the hydrangea.

Alastair Smithson

Pymers Mead

Dulwich

London SE21

December 2017

Dearest Monique,

I'd love to be able to see you again but I know we can't. I'm not even sure if you want to hear from me. I don't want you to reply or anything. It's just that I need to write.

Things haven't been going well. Denise and I broke up. The marriage didn't last. She is living in Bristol now with the kids. Yes, I have kids – Adrian and Cath, short for Catherine. I'd have liked you to have met them. They can be so beautiful. Cath gives a grin at times that reminds me of you.

Denise loved me when we married, but it always seemed a fantasy. One minute, she was infatuated with the man on the Board. The next, I'm disgusting. Yes, she found out. I couldn't let go of the letters I'd composed to you; they kept me together. They were in a box with my diary and old photo album, in the bottom drawer of my filing cabinet. She found the spare key. I didn't even know there was a spare key! We talked through everything. I thought we talked it out.

I'm not allowed to see the children now. Denise told the court all sorts of lies. It was horrible. I didn't help myself; I was angry; showing it in court is stupid. Denise kept her composure, looked the part throughout. What we did was discussed and extrapolated upon. I could never do the things they said. They threatened to call you as a witness; that's when I caved.

Adrian is five and Cath two. One minute I was the centre of their world. They are still the centre of mine. I still go through their toys, photos, and books: the football that Adrian once kicked over to our neighbour's. The smooth plastic doll in a green silk dresses that was Cath's. It relieves me up to a point, but it's only a temporary relief. I end up thinking, will I ever see them again? I have some quite destructive thoughts about the kids and me, and that's not so nice. I wish I was more confident in myself.

I did get on with Denise. She was good company on the whole. And, I didn't put up any resistance when she suggested moving to Dulwich. That was in August 2014. Yes, I have been materially very successful. It is a great place – a huge living area, wood-floored kitchen and three double bedrooms. I'm going to have to sell it now. I can't afford to live here any more. Adrian loved the garden. I put up a small goal for him. He would be Chelsea and rush around with a constant laugh, all energy, giving his whole being to the game. He was a pain though when Cath was born. He would pester us to sleep in Mummy and Daddy's bed. It is difficult to pacify a jealous four-year-old.

I miss them. Their noise. Their smells. Even Denise – even after what she put me through. She says she hates me. It doesn't stop her accepting my money though.

I feel lost, not sure what to do with myself. I feel as I felt back then. Nothing matters. But I don't want this ache. I feel so lonely without them. Without you.

This is the last letter I'm going to write to you.

I never had a chance to tell you how it felt being separated. You were a part of me – gone. I carried on working and showed off a respectable face. I immersed myself in the law. Funnily enough, that's probably why I did so well. But I haven't enjoyed myself. I wasn't able to give myself in to fun until after Adrian's birth. That was seven years without laughter. He gave me the miracle of my life as well as himself.

You told me you loved me once. That's still important to me. It is the only other important thing to have ever happened to me, along with the kids. I still love you. I've gone all blank. I'm embarrassed at invading your privacy.

I wish you 12 Happy Birthdays. 12 Christmases. 12 Happy New Years. The 5th September, our birthday, was always difficult. Denise never understood why I didn't want to celebrate.

I'm sure you have moved on, put me behind you, have a thriving family life, which does not need my interference. I feel embarrassed at invading your life after all this time. You probably don't want to hear from me at all, but I need to say you are important to me still. We are different people now, you and I. But it is just, I need to know, need to feel, you are still out there: Breathing. Alive. And, happy?

I hope one of us is happy. That would make me feel at least in some way complete. There is a constant need, something that's in my foundations. It's a companion, a constant emptiness. I didn't want to write that, but there it is in black and white. And, I don't know if I will ever hear from you again. Maybe after Mama and Papa are gone? I don't mean that in a bad way. I love them – even though I know they won't want my love. But who knows what the future will bring.

It seems like my punishment is to never be allowed a family life.

Love,

Ali Xxx

9. HABIT

Why do I do it? I always forget about the nausea that comes with the excitement. I've been doing this since I was fourteen. Back then, I hid what I was doing. I was ashamed at the prospect of being caught. That's seventy years ago; I still feel shame. It's a dirty habit.

Looking at the dark-haired girl reminds me of Annabel. I miss her. I want to give myself pleasure but all I'm feeling is loss. God took her away, you see. Sixteen years ago. And there has been a gap in my body since. I feel that emptiness needs to be filled.

The dark-haired girl is smiling at me. Annabel didn't have any of the risk factors: poor diet, smoker or high cholesterol. She was in great health; she did everything right. Here one moment, gone the next.

I can still taste gravy. I had poured it all over the new potatoes I had at lunch. I bought the Pukka steak pie (for one) cheap from Sainsbury's first thing this morning – it was going off today. There aren't any good places to eat out around here any more. You can't get a decent lunch. Nobody makes faggots or steak with kidney.

It's all Indian, Thai, Italian or Chinese. The local's gone too, not even a wine bar to replace it.

I look closer at this smiling girl – I'm aroused and depressed in equal measure. I flick through pictures. Annabel nearly caught me a couple of times; pretended she didn't know what I was doing. She definitely knew. She told me: 'All men do it!' The way she said it was so matter of fact. It didn't stop me feeling dirty though.

I was pleased to see the pie, with its yellow sticker, in the reduced section. My favourite is steak pie and boiled vegetables, followed by dessert. I remember the ad for cream cakes: 'Naughty but nice!' I stand up from my chair and move in real space; I feel the physicality of my body. I was strong when I was young but I have to be careful now – the body can end up hurting if I do a wrong move. In search of instant satisfaction, I walk to the kitchen and open the fridge; there's no pudding that might fill the hole. I could go to the sweet shop – it's only down the road. No, I can't be bothered. The man who runs it is foreign, from North India. He's a good one though. It's amazing, he stocks everything in there, you only have to ask. He was the one who sold me the bunting we put up, the year before Annabel died. But nobody really cared about the Golden Jubilee, not like the Silver Jubilee. Annabel and I went to a great street party back in 1977; there was no rationing; we ate well and I drunk too much. She scolded me for my appetite – I even miss that side of her.

I look in the cupboards; there is a twin park of caramel Hobnobs. It's a strain reaching for the nearer packet; I hope my shoulder's not going to hurt later. I consider making a cup of coffee, but taking the packet of biscuits to the computer seems more important than waiting for a kettle to boil.

On my return, I hear the computer's slight hum. I move the mouse and it makes a scuffing sound on the wood table as the screen lights up. I stare at the screen and stop noticing the sounds.

The images on display are sexy in ways I could never have imagined when I was young. The foreign ways aren't all bad. Our laws used to try to prevent this sort of thing coming into the country. The specialist magazines found a way to still get in from Europe, like everything else, bloody EEC.

They got rid of our pounds and ounces, feet and inches. Next it would have been miles and the pound – if we hadn't stopped them! Nobody seems to care any more that we fought these people when I was a child. How can we trust them? We were a great nation once, we ruled the world, we won wars. But now ... it's all coloureds and liberals.

Computers are marvellous: they show everything! The image of a woman with her hand on a young man's parts flashes across the screen. We weren't allowed to see that erect, in the old days.

I go back to the dark-haired girl to get aroused again. She is about the same age as Annabel was when I met her at a party in the Officer's Mess. I wasn't an officer. It was Hamish Anderson's nineteenth birthday. Somehow he had talked Captain Marsh into letting him use it. Hamish could talk the hind legs off a donkey. I wonder what he is doing now? I've not seen him in decades. I hope he's still alive. We have shared history. I'd like him still to be out there.

It was just after the Queen's coronation. The room was still done out in red, white and blue paper-chains and there was a large picture of Her Majesty on the wall. For music, I remember: Benny Goodman, Glenn Miller and Bing Crosby. There was limited party food; I ate a sausage roll and two small corned beef sandwiches. My attention wasn't on the food.

Most of the men, like me, were in uniform. Annabel was out of uniform wearing a brown silk top and a long fawn skirt; her hair was in a bun. I never tired of seeing Annabel with her hair up in a bun – it is such a classy look. The first time I saw her she was with two other women dancing around three glasses of punch. That night, I was on the Double Diamond, or should I say Dutch courage.

Hamish introduced us. I gained confidence as she took an interest in what I said. I challenged her to a game of billiards, which she accepted saying: 'I'm not very good.' The table was pretty decent. I tossed a coin and she called heads correctly. She chalked the tip of her cue, concentrated to aim her cue and dead-on connected the white ball with the red with her opening stroke; she didn't look so bad. I took my turn then stood back to survey how the balls had fallen. I watched her bending over before she took her next shot. I had to draw my mind to the game. We chatted as we played. I didn't say anything at first when she fouled by pocketing the cue ball, then I simply stated: 'It happens to everyone.' I won and asked 'as a prize' if I could see her again. It was simpler back then. Nothing like my encounters with women nowadays; except when I've paid.

The Freedom Pass is good. All the young have Oyster cards or contactless … I've been told paying by card is safer in the shops. I'll never use a contactless card. You don't know where you are! The kids don't understand money. They're spoilt. In my day, we served our country, we had discipline. Discipline is out of fashion now. No one shows any respect. Marriage is no longer for life. It was right for us. Annabel and I, for life.

But … I feel heavy in myself; I don't want this feeling. I start to cram biscuits into my mouth. I'm weary. I can taste chocolate, oats and toffee-goo. It's sweet and …

I've had to pay for it, mostly. That's what the women in front of me are. They do it for the money. A physical act – it is just two animals. They would only do it for money. I can feel myself getting aroused and upset. I feel bad but can't stop myself. My leg is shaking and it's only partly sexual.

Annabel and I got married in May 1957 and our first home was in Clerkenwell. The neighbourhood was full of Italians. Little Italy they called it. Religious people the Italians, they all went to mass at St Peter's. Their food was good once you got used to it: pizza, pasta or whatever it was that Annabel brought back from the deli. They have gone from Clerkenwell now. It's like everything, all gone – only to be seen on the History Channel from satellite TV. Satellite TV!

Click, click, clicking the mouse, I move through the pictures faster. A peroxide blonde with a muscular black man is replaced by another blonde getting wet in a car wash.

I look over to the picture on the mantelpiece. There is Annabel and I at Hamish's wedding in 1959. We are smiling, looking forward to a bright future. And there is another dark-haired girl in front of me on the screen. It is good to have a warm feeling in my groin and the sweet and velvety taste in my mouth. I call out: 'An …'

After the moment my mouth and sacs are left empty. I am confused, disjointed and weak. I turn the computer off and my flat seems very quiet.

10. THE PLANET HAS LIMITS

Euston being shut was a real inconvenience for Jerome, as it was for his fellow commuters. *Unusual weather pattern for this time of year.*

There was the scuffle of feet and a tourist with a noisy roller suitcase followed close behind for five minutes. He found the noise irritating. The increased crowds on the slippery pavement of the Euston Road meant people pushed up against each other. A woman wrapped in an expensive-looking red woollen coat was far too close to him as she shouted into an iPhone: 'I'm running late ... Bloody trains!' Her red coat touched him and Jerome smelt the woman's overbearing perfume.

I've got to be careful. I don't want to stumble into a random stranger. Carrying a new black briefcase, he made his way with cautious steps the third of a mile to Warren Street station. With only a few hundred yards to go, a group of office workers, all male, were about to push past him, he stopped. *Bloody people! I don't want to fall and touch the ground.*

At Warren Street, Jerome put on a new mask before

descending on the escalator. *I know escalators have been responsible for severe injuries and even a few deaths.* He spread his feet and braced his legs to create as strong a stance as he could, anything to avoid the handrail. *That rubber is touched by everyone.* He kept his hand hovering above.

A man with a small rucksack, wearing a smart shirt and tie, walked past and squeezed into the gap in the steps directly in front of him. *He's too close! His hair is clean but the back of his neck has two angry pimples.* The man sniffed and pulled a handkerchief from his pocket. *Cough, colds, Covid and flu are winter illnesses.* The man walked down the last steps. At the bottom of the escalator the man disappeared into the crowd.

Jerome followed the signs for the Victoria line southbound. He waited on a packed platform. The train pulled in and Jerome got on. He managed to get a seat. *That's the first good thing to happen to me today.* The woman beside him didn't look up from the game on her mobile – tiny rainbow-coloured shapes were cascading down the screen: *modern communication or rather lack of it!*

He lifted *The Guardian* from his briefcase; he placed the case on his lap with the newspaper rested on top. *Looking the part for clients is no justification for this leather case; why did I buy it? The old one could have lasted at least another year.* Jerome leant his wrist, with a silver-plated sportsman's watch, over the top of the newspaper.

He closed his eyes: *The enclosed space of an underground carriage is a subterranean world, separated from nature; no one can tell it is mid-winter.* Jerome heard a rustle and opened his eyes.

A little girl, with her mother, pulled open a blue bag of Walkers' crisps. *I can smell the unmistakable synthetic pong of cheese and onion.* The mother coughed. *She didn't even put up her hand to protect others. People cough and infect everyone else through air droplets. There are thousands of germs and viruses out here. None of the vaccines are effective.*

The girl crunched her way through her crisps. The sound was drowned out as the train rattled though the tunnel. There was a little relative calm as the train slowed on its approach to Oxford Circus. The doors opened and there was chatter, more coughs and footsteps as people exit and enter. The mother and daughter disembarked.

Jerome opened his *Guardian* to an article entitled: Ten ways to make Britain a more green and pleasant land. The 1962 quote from Rachel Carson struck him: *'Humankind is challenged, as it has never been challenged before, to prove its maturity and its mastery – not of nature, but of itself.'* He huddled behind the paper.

A man, dressed in black coat, jeans, T-shirt and skull and crossbones mask, sat down next to him. *It wasn't long ago when everyone wore a mask.* The man put on full ear-covering headphones; Jerome recognised them as sound deadening. *People want to cut out the problems of the world!* As the train pulled out of Oxford Circus, the man blew cool air at himself using his Skyocean personal fan. Jerome looked up from his newspaper, trying not to show discontent.

He went back to reading about how habitat and biodiversity loss was increasing the likelihood of pandemics. *We suffer when the world's ecosystems suffer. God! The hum from that fan is annoying.* At Green Park he gave up trying to read, carefully folded his newspaper and put it back into his briefcase. *Another transitory item! At least, I will put this paper into the recycling later. We've all got to try our best.* The man with a personal fan got off at Victoria.

After the train pulled out of Victoria, Jerome shut his eyes again. He counted the going in and coming out of the next two stations: *One Pimlico ... Two Vauxhall.*

As the train slowed for Stockwell, Jerome opened his eyes and stood up.

The train jolted and he had to hold on to a handrail to steady himself. *Yuck! I don't touch things in public places!*

The doors opened. Jerome got off to change on to the Northern Line; home was further south. He walked the short distance to the right platform. Jerome saw from a digital display board that the train to Morden was three minutes away. As he waited, there was an announcement: 'We'll sort it. See it, say it, sorted'. *They are saying the same thing twice! We'll sort ... sorted.*

The tube arrived and a group of people – three men and a woman – got on with Jerome. All four were unmasked.

Sitting down again, Jerome reached for an antibacterial gel from his briefcase. *This'll have to do until I can wash my hands.* He rubbed his hands with gel.

One of the men had sat directly opposite; he grabbed a hamburger from a McDonald's brown paper bag and gorged. *As the sickly smell has reached my nostrils, I know grease particles have entered my body.*

The woman, who sat at a little distance from the three men, plonked down her large handbag on the seat and took out a pink make-up bag. She started to apply eyeliner. Jerome looked away. *That's dangerous. What if the train jolted?* When he turned his head back she was powdering her cheeks. *My eye is itchy but I'm not going to scratch it. It's no good touching your face.*

Once the man had finished his McDonald's, he scrunched up the paper bag and left it with the waste burger box and red and yellow fries carton on the seat beside him. *Am I invisible? Openly littering directly in front of me. This man must think himself so important he has a right to litter up the public space! Why doesn't he just keep hold of his rubbish, leave it in his own pocket, until he is beside a bin later?* Jerome wanted to say something but he was scared because there were three men. He tried to self-justify: *Familiarity with anybody in a public place is bad since they are invariably close enough to spread infections.* A few minutes later, Jerome caught a glimpse of himself reflected in the carriage window, behind the man's head. His friends had told him he was handsome in an unconventional way – with green eyes, a tidy beard and an earring. He looked away. *I'm ashamed I didn't say anything.*

With her make-up put away in her handbag, the woman laughed at the men's jokes. They were now vying for her attention.

The man opposite picked up a discarded copy of the *Metro* free paper. *Free! It's manufactured. Energy is used. Pollution created. We all pay!* But the man didn't read the *Metro*, he placed it over his rubbish, as if to hide the detritus. At the same time, he shared a joke with his friends.

Jerome was disgusted all over again: *It's even worse that you know what you have done is wrong!* Jerome stared at the side of the man's head;

he wanted to make him feel some shame for what had now been purposefully made into an 'out of sight/out of mind' crime. Jerome felt alert, ready for action. *The planet is going to hell because of Homo sapiens. Eight billion and counting. But hey, it's out of sight ... Oh, no, it isn't! The ecological catastrophe predicted for the last sixty years has arrived. It is staring us in the face. Man-made climate change is here; the unusual cold spell is erratic weather.*

At Clapham Common, the three men and woman stood up to disembark. Jerome stared at the man who had left the rubbish. *We cut down the rainforests and consume the finite resources so our nearest and dearest can have all the consumer products they want. Right now, we are missing doing so much that would contribute towards saving our planet.*

Jerome checked his own thoughts and recognised it was himself that was unusual – the man's attitude was the norm. With the depressing thought *humanity is doomed,* came, for Jerome, an unexpected carefree feeling. He travelled on to Balham. *Without memory you don't see change. People forget how it was so quickly.* He walked from the station. Being at ease didn't last long.

At home, after taking the newspaper out, he left his briefcase and shoes by the front door. He went into the kitchen to put the paper in the recycling. He washed his hands, with a smear of eco-detergent off the cap, before taking his mask off and disposing of it in the bin. He felt tired so, as a pick me up, drank a half-glass of cold water – it didn't work. Beaten by sadness, he went to the lounge and lay down on the sofa: *I thought my efforts would make things better.*

11. NEW BEGINNING

Jerome has little idea about his own looks; good or bad. His thoughts are filled by more serious matters. *I was at primary school in the 1960s, the first time we witnessed our precious planet as a whole, photographed from space.* He feels alive as he walks on pavement made of slabs of concrete. *The lights in the town nightscape are quite beautiful. The cool air is free of germs.* He tries to ignore the slogans, graffiti and tags sprawled over a concrete wall: *Tonight, I don't want to engage with the marginalised shouting for attention.*

He relaxes into his stride. *There was a time when I was up on stage at the Waterloo Action Centre. It was crowded but important so my nerves didn't faze me. I pontificated about finite resources, fish with tumours and the end of the world. You were in the audience agreeing and empathising. But I didn't see you, I just saw a sea of faces. Faces who needed to be converted to the Green agenda. At the end, a man in a bobble hat asked questions. On global warming, I said something like: 'The first goodbyes will be to the small island nations and southern Bangladesh.' On biodiversity I replied: 'I think the complex interactions of wonderous creatures in nature is something to be celebrated.' You approached me afterwards in your hijab and with your humble handshake. Still, I didn't see you, my eyes closed to everything but saving the Earth.*

Up ahead, Jerome sees a group of lads and subconsciously tries to look more confident, cocky, not someone to be messed with. He exaggerates the effect of his rubber-soled shoes to give a bounce to each of his steps. He twists slightly at the hips so the top half of his body bobs leftward and back.

Going past, he sees the lads' clothes are all in extra bright colours, as if to say: 'Here I am!' against the huge man-made structures, the advertising, the people and noise of an anonymous modern city: *Their statement is about as effective as dropping a sugar cube into the sea.*

Was my preaching any more effective? I tried to tell them what they needed to hear. Most reacted badly to my challenge; they only wanted to hear what they already believed. The majority had already embraced the sweet lies, adopted faith in consumerism and technological fixes.

Over the road is an ex-local authority housing block. In front, a girl in biker boots that are huge compared to her legs. As Jerome moves closer, he can see the metal plate on the front has never felt the rub of a bike chain, she wears a red remembrance poppy attached sideways to the arm of her black jacket and has the brightest of red lips. She crosses the road at exactly the same time as him going in the opposite direction; there were no cars in either direction but she trots across, just in case. *Maybe it was my presence that sped her on?*

On passing the housing block, a baby's disposable nappy is

thrown from a high flat. *I suppose that's meant for the street.* It lands upside down on the bonnet of a blue Mini. Little browny-green turds splatter the paint work. Jerome stops. *Disgusting! So unhygienic!* He gulps air deeply. *Should I do something? Complain? I could ring the door bell, if I knew which one it was. I've got to do something, if only I knew what?*

Jerome turns away; there is a discarded Tesco's carrier bag and an empty Coca-Cola bottle on the pavement. *I see waste everywhere!*

All my life, I've felt anxiety about the damage we do to the environment. Guilt for climate change. Shame for biodiversity loss. Why can't others see the destruction of habitat increases zoonotic viruses? Why can't we work with nature, not against it? … Is environmentalism my religion? There is plastic everywhere; I once tried to stop using it. I fail and fail and fail again.

He walks past a poster peeling off a billboard and is distracted by the slogan that promises a better life. *Anyone who repetitively tells you what you want to hear is untrustworthy. Follow them for closure of thought.*

He walks through an alley. *I need to do more … I need to block the negative and focus on spreading positivity into the world. The 1970s brought Friends of the Earth, Greenpeace and World Wildlife Fund. The 1980s saw battles won to save the whale and stop CFCs making a bigger hole in the ozone layer.*

He walks on. *I have slogged through life. I have done many good deeds: trying to heal those who were ill; trying to help those who needed help. There is always more to do.*

Did I fight for false certainty? Desperately tried harder to create something pure? But the desire to push forward stems from a weakness to accept what is there in front of me.

I feel like I am dying. I tried telling the truth and ended up alone. I don't want to be on my own.

We hardly exchanged twenty words but you remain with me; beautiful in a hijab. Your handshake was humble – your darkened eyes weren't.

Jerome comes to a weather-worn sign that read CLOSED. The tarmac path ahead is chained-off. On the other side, the path leads to trees into a darkened park. Jerome has questions: *I could ignore this sign and carry on anyway? I should do what I'm told, shouldn't I? Most people do what they're told – it's obvious – follow the leader. The lads wore the bright uniform of their gang, while everyone else wears the same looking clothes in the same dull colours and fashions. They all do what others want – conform to the norm. Maybe that is why so many people don't like seeing women in burqas or hijabs? It cheers me up. It's like when I see a punk or an unconvincing crossdresser. None of it does anyone any harm, does it? It's something a little bit different. What is it that stops people celebrating the complex interactions of the wonderous in nature?*

Without thinking about the consequences, Jerome clambers over the chained-off gate. *Your hair was covered but I remember your black eyebrows; if you removed your hijab, it would have been the blackest of hair that escaped.* A gust of air brings fresh smells. *Let's go see …*

From the path he moves to scrub-grass and weed underfoot. Then he is surrounded by dark green, with tints of new purple, nature as he walks into the park. He is careful to avoid treading on any of the spring crocuses.

12. TIME TRAVEL

I had once wanted to make my mark on the world; but, not anymore! After two nervous breakdowns and five years' unemployment I finally gave up. My mind now told me I would never achieve anything. Anything of great importance, that is. And, to justify this change of heart I said to myself: *What is the point anyway, life is without meaning, we all die in the end and everything we do turns to dust.*

I no longer looked after myself. I sat staring into space or at the wall: I stopped washing and eating. I lost all ability to communicate with others.

My family were concerned and took me to the local medical practice. My general practitioner told me, 'Eddie, you must take an antidepressant, paroxetine, once a day. It's a selective serotonin reuptake inhibitor.' I must have looked none the wiser, as he added: 'There will be more serotonin in your brain and therefore, chemically, it should cheer you up.'

In the interim, waiting for the drug to start to work, I went and lived with my mother to look after me. After a month in the old family home surroundings, I began to start feeling more myself again and to go on a daily walk, starting at 12.45 precisely. While walking, I would daydream: *What if I had everything ... ten billion pounds ... All science in my hands ... What if I could travel backwards and forwards in time?*

On Tuesday 23rd May, an old man stood on the pavement directly in front of me blocking my path. This man had appeared to me twice before. Previously when I'd mentioned him, my psychiatrist told me 'You may have been confused by a stranger. You might have just been seeing things.' The old man again wore what looked like a Lycra body stocking, a belt with things hanging off it, dark glasses and a bowl-like hat on his head. He spoke, 'Hello, Eddie James.'

I broke out in a sweat all over. It wasn`t this stranger's dress that disturbed me; there was something in his face that reminded me of my grandfather. And, both previous times after he had appeared I had ended up getting more and more excited. In retrospect, I understood how my erratic behaviour drew the attention of the authorities. The doctors called it hyper-mania and used physical restraints and tranquillizers to calm me down. Seeing the man, today, made me tense. I did not want the same things to happen again. I was bewildered: *I mustn't believe in this man ... He doesn`t exist. No, it is impossible! This man reminds me ... of myself.*

The old man continued to talk, 'Don`t be frightened or alarmed. I am your future. I am you.' He began fading before my very eyes and thrust a newspaper into my hands. 'We haven`t much time. Make some real money. We will die if you don't believe in me.' *This is all too ridiculous. I'm hearing the voice of a ghost. I must be going mad again.*

The old man disappeared fully.

Whilst walking slowly onwards, I tried to understand what had just happened. *I had contemplated time travel and I had then seemingly talked to a biologically older version of myself. The old man disappeared leaving me with … I* looked down at the newspaper. *Nothing unusual, but surely today is the 23rd, not … Tomorrow's newspaper! Which is disintegrating in my hands. Bollocks – it's crumbling!*

Paper flakes fell from the edges of the newspaper towards the pavement. They disappeared before landing, like snow trying to settle on warm ground. Quickly, I turned to the back pages. I had enough time to see the winners at Kempton Park: in the 2.30 it was River Boy, the 3.30 Pork Pie and 4.45 Heart of a Penitent's Rose. It was a shower of paper until the final piece became dust and then nothing; as if the paper had never existed.

I was confused as to what to do. I didn`t want to return to a mental hospital. While at Bellamore, my psychiatrist had strongly advised me: 'If you see the old man again, that indicates a breakdown is starting to happen. Come and see me immediately!' *Perhaps I should ignore the old man, my old self.* My psychiatrist had said I could 'come in for a rest' and take the stabilizer drug lithium, as a preventative measure 'for the rest of your life'. The idea of permanently putting drugs into my body was unappealing.

I'm not sure about this other stuff; the old man is so weird. I was just daydreaming, wasn't I? But what had the old man said? We could die! I wondered: *When he said 'believe in me' did he mean if I believe in the day-dream it would be true? I could put a bet on the horses to find out if he was real or not?*

But then, maybe, I don't want to know, I don't want to risk losing my mind.

My body walked me into a betting shop and I put a £20 tri-cast on my three horses. At 5-1, 33-1, and 28-1 my accumulator bet, on the nose, worked out at 4,620-1.

Incredibly, by 5pm I had won £92,400. Which must have pissed off Mr Will Hill behind the till. The betting shop manager told me head office would do the large payment. Leaving the shop, the old 'stranger' reappeared smiling, as somehow I expected he would.

I told him: 'I don't want to believe in you. It only leads to trouble.'

He laughed. 'Since you believed in *yourself* we now have a chance of survival.' He handed me three A4 booklets and told me to go and get the invention ideas they contained first patented and then built. 'The first invention can be strictly hired out at an exorbitant rate.'

When I got home that evening, my mother said: 'You look cheery.'

'I had a win on the horses.'

'When did you start gambling?'

'Today.'

She looked at me suspiciously.

'When I get my hands on the cash, I'd like to give you £20,000. As you have always looked after —'

She held up a hand. 'I don't need it son, I have this property.' She gestured with both her hands all around before asking: 'What is going on?'

I told her about the old man, the winnings and my worries

about my mental health.

She was slow in considering her response. 'It is difficult to disagree with £93,400 … If you don't know what to do, son, make the machines and go and see your psychiatrist for care as well.'

It was good advice – not that I took it in full.

Arranging a number of practical matters came first: I set up 'Regress Tech Co' at Companies House. After replacing the invention titles on the front covers of the booklets with their initials to disguise the contents, I made a visit to a photocopier. I paid for three submissions at the Patent Office.

I then rang Eastbank University. On pick up, I asked: 'Is that the secretary to the Head of the Physics Department?'

'Yes.'

'I'd like to arrange an appointment with Dean Appleby to discuss making a small grant for research.'

'When would you be available to meet?'

An appointment was fixed for the next Tuesday.

*

Dean Appleby was a pleasant man of short stature, who wore a dark-brown suit and a brown tie, which tried to escape from his shirt collar every time he expressed himself with jerky mannerisms. He reminded me of a ferret.

I showed him a diagram for the 'S.T.' that resembled two hats attached to each other by a piece of string. He studied it in a perplexed manner, told me it looked clever but didn't understand what it did. I too had little idea what this thing would do. I avoided answering a question by saying, 'I'd like the work to be kept as confidential as possible … I have £45,000, could you build this machine for me?' *I was sceptical but I felt I had nothing to lose. The money had come from nowhere. I'd decided I would use half of the winnings.*

Without batting an eyelid, he said: 'Of course, I can get one of our PhD students on to it immediately, some are looking for projects with money attached; not many grants available nowadays. But I can`t promise it will do whatever it is meant to do.' Neither could I.

Mrs Julie Greene headed up the work. For the next year, I got phone calls and letters from Eastbank research scientists, of increasing seniority, telling me that this had led to that discovery, which was always 'absolutely amazing!'

Finally, they had completed the first 'Subconscious Telephone': A mechanism which I knew was supposed to help the two participants wearing the hats to communicate/interact with the other through the 'piece of string'.

Being the owner of this new technology, I was asked if I wanted to be the first guinea pig. I agreed. I didn't expect it to work in any major way.

Mrs Julie Greene turned out to be a rather pleasant PhD student. She wore a navy top with jeans, with spectacles on her nose, while the scarf over her shoulder had a snake print design. As she had started and carried out most of the work, she was the other participant.

We put on the hats and the machine was turned on. It was very strange. We entered each other's minds. It was like being and looking in a mirror, which I, or the other (Julie in this case), could choose to learn from and use if we so wished. I gave her the ability to see herself through my eyes, and she must have allowed me to see myself through her`s. Then our minds merged. I knew all about her husband. She knew about my succession of failed relationships: Kay, Tess and Olivia. All my and her secrets, shames and guilts seemed trivial to our collective mind. *Whole at last!* Our faults so minor. We liked ourself. *How lovely it feels!* I became aroused, or did she? The female body placed her left foot back and her right foot forward then swayed her body back and forth. We were both surprised by the unexpected sensual pleasure of being in each other`s bodies. The male body was very still but breathing heavily. Neither of us could hide the desire from our single mind.

We felt, with our hands. But these female hands were mine and they were on a woman`s body, *my female body!* I was engulfed by Julie`s pleasure at arousing a male body. We felt the stroke of hands. Without shame, we masturbated, or was it sex we shared? I don`t know.

The subconscious telephone had a safety feature. Without it, Julie and I wouldn't have ever wanted or even contemplated being disconnected from each other. The machine was set with an upper time limit of sixty minutes' use, then it automatically cut off communication.

When the hour was up, I felt torn apart. Back as a man, my stomach cramped. *How incredibly lonely it feels!*

The hats were taken off and then Julie and I held each other in our arms. When we talked, she said: 'I feel sick.' I felt it too. We were feeling the same loss from our broken connection. *I have felt broken for so long, it seemed unfair to have the fleeting completeness taken away in an hour.*

On reflection, the automatic cut off was a sensible feature; with prolonged use, neither of us would have seen ourselves as separate entities any more. The machine made the dream of being whole a reality, and then destroyed it. The machine also never allowed the same two people ever to be connected up again after the once.

Julie told me she was 'confused' and 'felt unfaithful' before she went back to her husband. Two days after our separation, she told me, 'I'm working to rekindle our marriage.' I felt lost in her words. That was not what I wanted to hear, even if it was morally the right thing to do.

It emotionally hurt me some more, the next day, when she added: 'The use of the "telephone" will help John and I to open up and share with each other again.' I had to suppress anger: *I didn't approve that usage.*

As for me, for a couple of months, I mourned her loss acutely. The first two weeks were the worst. I kept dry retching and couldn`t properly eat. The emotional pain eventually passed, helped by me using the machine again, a new person filling the void. However much I shared myself with another, coming out of the connected state always felt terrible. The more I, or anyone else, used it, the less intense and more comfortable we became with the joy and tears it brought. What I had had with Julie, my first, always felt special. I wondered if we would ever get back together again?

My mental health improved. I realised the long-term effect of the mind-meld was positive on my psyche. I decided to stop all medications: *I don't need them.* I should have talked to my psychiatrist beforehand, but I had something to prove: *It's my mind and so it's my choice.*

I hadn't thought through the full implications for society of the new technology, I just brought it to market. There was an outcry at first by people frightened of ever revealing their true multi-faceted contradictory selves. I read some terrible stories in the papers. But over time, like the impact on me, people found the machines beneficial. After the initial shock when using it, most felt happier with themselves and not so worried about being definitely sure about things. I noticed people became far more tolerant of other`s differences, recognising something of themselves in everyone. I felt proud of my part in making this change happen.

The machine was a great commercial success. Regress Tech Co. started making a lot of money. As suggested in the 'S.T.' notebook, we had always insisted on a waiver before use. Some people were unable to cope with the powerful insights the machine brought out; damage could be permanent. The revelations about the thoughts of our 'human too' religious and political leaders were often disputed. I should never have allowed its use for interrogation purposes.

I gave the go-ahead and project numbers two and three began. From the profits Regress Tech Co. made, I ploughed money back into the science departments at Eastbank; a vast array of the top scientists could be afforded. My lawyers drew up a novel employment contract for all to sign; it stipulated that their thoughts would become the property of Regress Tech.

Working on the two projects, my scientists made discovery after discovery. World scientific progress seemed to be centred on our researchers and their work. And this progress was rapidly speeding up.

Mother died and my depression re-emerged. I was so worried I went to see my psychiatrist. He was retired, an old man now. I had to pay for a private appointment. He told me: 'It is quite natural to feel sad with bereavement … Kübler-Ross believed there are non-linear stages to grief. You might experience other emotions.'

'Not even *she* stayed with me!'

'Why do you say "Not even she stayed with you?" That's unusual.'

'I have had a problem with unrequited love. I'm shy with women. When I fall for someone, I get far too emotional. It puts them off. They never stay around long. Now even mother has left me.'

'You have your memories of your mother …'

'Yes … and mother left me her house. Neither of these things are what I need.'

He asked: 'Are you angry?'

I ended the first private session at this point. The power dynamic, as I employed him, was far superior than when he worked for the NHS.

Invention number two required intensive work from the Eastbank biology department to create technology that would keep human tissue alive. The basic idea was a biological extension of the 'subconscious telephone' using a spider's web network of inputs held together by cytoskeletons made of a protein-based scaffold similar to that which holds human cells together. When invention two was only half-built, it gave the scientists a new means of mass communication, the ability of group thought.

Eastbank turned to me and the machine in its decision-making. I was co-opted on to the university's senate.

Julia and her team worked on invention three. As I was often on campus, I kept running into her. I felt a thrill each time I saw her. I realised I wanted Mrs Julie Greene for myself. I invited her for a coffee and she accepted.

Over cappuccinos, I felt excitement when I told her: 'You are looking well.'

'You too.'

'It's weird isn't it, only seeing the outside of each other ...'

'Yes, I guess,' was all she replied.

'I wonder ... I know I still feel ...' I struggled with my words. 'Do you still feel the connection between us?' I could see in her face she knew my intention.

'Eddie, don't!'

'I can't help myself thinking about a future with you. As companions.'

'You know I'm trying to make the best of my marriage.'

I wanted to say something romantic. 'I can offer so much more ... you know that. You know me.'

This time she chose to reject me.

I tried dating other women. The beautiful, gold-digging Jessica was the longest lasting, at less than a month. Basically dating was a failure as none of the women were Julie.

It took only seven more years for Julia and her team to make invention three, a matter transformer. Like a magic wand with one wave, the position of atoms in molecules could be altered. Matter, or energy, couldn`t be created or destroyed, but substances could be altered. At last, waste could be converted back into useful material. I bought up all the landfill sites I could. Nobody turned down my offer to pay for mankind`s waste. And the rubbish became riches.

At the ex-landfill sites, I converted the larger holes, that had been used to house waste, into vast underground complexes. Artificial sunlight was installed, gardens planted and life grew. The biggest complexes were populated until they were thriving underground towns. I set aside a number of the smaller complexes.

Being unfeasibly wealthy, I could have anything money could buy. But money cannot buy everything. I couldn't have Julie or bring back my mother.

I went to see my psychiatrist again and talked about Julie: 'She wouldn't come to me.'

'It sounds a bit like you want revenge,' he said.

'No.'

'We need to talk about your anger towards women.'

'No.'

As I was paying, saying 'No' really meant no, but that didn't stop me thinking about his words. Rather than anger, after Julie had rejected me, I knew I had to set her free to be with and love the other.

I told my psychiatrist, 'I will be dealing with my anger towards women.'

He said: 'That's good ... that sounds good.'

Money and knowledge had brought to me great power which I now wielded. I had been rejected by so many women in my past. I had loved them but this love had not been reciprocated. I felt they had imprisoned a part of me. It was time to give pay back for my unrequited love. Vengeance would be mine. I sentenced each of them to a 'paradise'. In the smaller complexes, I imprisoned these women to a life in her own underground Garden of Eden. Each 'Eve' (Kay, Tess, Olivia and Jessica) was kept totally alone except for her flowers, vegetables and animals.

This was not Mrs Julie Greene's fate. She had loved me as I loved her! I wanted to lift her on to a pedestal. I'd do anything for her.

A decade later, Julie's husband and my psychiatrist had died. I was no longer boyish; I was not even mid-life anymore; there were too many lines and blemishes on my face; my hair was thin and grey. I asked Julie to accompany me to a luxury work conference.

She declined: 'I'm still mourning John.'

I told myself if I really love her she shall be free to live her life however she chooses.

Another prison was created. One complex was for a harem of females; to be my play-things – for amusement. This was for beautiful girls born and grown inside one of the many complexes, they knew no other life. They were to never know that the parameters on this life, that I'd given them, wasn't right and proper. There was a clear hierarchy to ensure order and compliance. Since birth, all desires, bar pleasing me, were subdued. My pleasure gave significance to these women's lives; it was what they were born for, and after many years of servitude would die for.

During this period the older man reappeared again. His body now resembled a black shield, its shadow arresting all warmth from the sun. His head hung down low. He could have been black cloaked and holding a scythe; the skeletal form with decaying flesh smiled at me with its skull-like head. Involuntarily I shivered.

His face sat formless; like a doll's head misshapen by heat, the plastic had dripped and flowed until all features were erased, but his lips moved, 'I have come as a warning of the distraction caused by your carnal desires, of complacency ...' From behind a locked window, I could hear the wind blowing outside. His face was inhuman as if yellow greaseproof paper had simply been wrapped around a skull. 'You are forgetting this could be the end for you and I; it is annihilation if you don't hurry up, we shall die!'

As the old man disappeared, I knew his words were highly significant. I remembered his previous appearances and disappearances, but this time it was a sobering. I had been distracted, by my desires, from keeping myself alive. Of course, questions went through my head; I wondered whether immortality was even possible. Then came resolve: I have to give it a go. Try my best.

Our progress was getting faster but we had to accelerate, I had to push for more.

*

I was getting older and older; thirty years had passed since the old man had given me the newspaper. Most of the original Eastbank scientists were now old or dying; a few were dead. The thoughts their brains contained were the property of Regress Tech Co. I put out an order: 'Keep the brains alive and make a very generous payoff to the next of kin.' We did not have to give any compensation but I wanted to smooth over any potential problems.

I needed to speed up scientific advancement. I began to buy, or if need-be steal, other great thinkers' brains.

Invention two was connected to the dead`s brains, the idea being to make one huge mind that could mine and sieve data from the connected AIs. This bio-computer meant scientific progress took another quantum leap forward. The world`s scientific establishment was unable to keep up or even understand the outpourings of my bio-computer. We fed it with more and more human brains. Even when her body died, Mrs Julie Greene's brain went in; *people I love always leave me;* but I was pleased this small part of her would stay with me. With a life of its own, the giant brain swelled and grew in size and knowledge.

Science had slowed the ageing process. But all that meant was my new fate was to die slowly. I asked myself, how can I stop dying of old age? I needed to be able to regress the ageing process.

I was called a transhumanist, trying to outrun death. Well, I wasn't trying to make myself into a machine, but the second part was true.

It was at the age of 117 that I was told theoretically we had the ability to go back in time. I demanded: 'Build me this time machine.'

*

Once what I called 'invention 4' was complete, I brought in the best team of doctors I could find to oversee my use of it. For the dry run, I stretched a specially made clingy-material stocking over my body. Other protective items of dress, against low-level radiation, included glasses and a helmet. I stood in the machine and it was turned on.

At first contact, unfortunately, all I told my younger self was: 'One, two, three ... testing.' The experience was physically exhausting.

The leading doctor told me: 'You are a frail man. The use of this machine will kill you. I advise only to use it sparingly, if at all.'

The second time in the time machine was frustrating. I tried to leaves clues to my younger self but he didn't understand what was going on. He kept saying 'You're not real! You're not real!' This drew the attention of a mental health team.

I realised I was going in too early. The time co-ordinates were shifted.

For the third contact, I hung a bag off my belt to hold the booklets containing two machine designs in as simple scientific language as possible. This trip went well; I successfully passed on the vital information.

From then on, progress was good but not good enough. I was still dying, I realised I had to go back another time to save us. I thought if my younger self saw me dying it would focus his mind on that task. The fourth contact was a great success at speeding him on.

I had reached the point where I had the ability to break the Laws of Physics. I could go back in time. But it wasn't time travel that I needed but to be able to regress ageing. I would then be immortal. I could live forever.

I went to see my later distracted self to tell me: 'It is annihilation if you don't hurry up.' He got the message - it pushed things forward but it still wasn't enough.

To have enough time to survive until I could, break the Laws of Nature, there was only one option left open to me – I had to speed up the progression of science even faster: Sixth contact.

Faster scientific progress linked to the faster time travel forward, like being propelled by a catapult, would mean I could outrun time; unless I was killed in the journey. I decided on one last trip to a mid-time range. All the doctors told me not to do any more time travel.

I nudged the co-ordinates back a little bit earlier. I put a copy of the newspaper (24th May) into the bag held by the belt around my waist. *That should convince him. He can start the work earlier with real money.* I got into my transporter; I knew I needed the progression of science so much better and sooner. Progress needed to speed up the acceleration forward. I switched on my time machine. I must break Nature. The Laws that will never be broken. Being flung forward into the past there was an almighty bang. Am I God? Am I Mad?

*

There I am walking aimlessly, young and disillusioned. I see a myriad of opportunities for my naive young self: lives I have not lived.

I am going to speak but I don't. The smell of freshly mown

grass distracts me. Then I feel both the sun and cool air on my face. These are pleasant sensations.

I watch the young man as he strolls past me. His shoulders are slouched; his face is sallow.

I look down at the newspaper in my hands, it begins to fragment. I let a flake drop towards the ground.

Before I turn to dust, let me savour a few brief moments of freedom – a freedom I have not before let myself enjoy – the freedom to fritter away time.

13. *COOL* BRITANNIA

A low babble of voices fills the pub.

Under a poster of Winston Churchill smoking a cigar, Dad – in one of his knock-off blue Aertex shirts with croc logo – sits in a wood-panelled alcove at a wooden round table. There is a large open cardboard box at his feet with miniature red buses, red phone boxes and Union flags inside.

At the jukebox, as my fingers hesitate over the buttons, I see how nicotine-stained they are. I choose to put on UB40. The song starts and I hear Ali Campbell singing.

Returning to Dad, I'm singing along: 'I'm a British subject —'

'Be proud of your roots,' he says, raising his glass.

I sit down alongside him, so he can hear me clearly: 'Greg committed suicide.'

'Who?'

'You know Greg. The man who kept on about the Falklands war.'

Dad pales momentarily. 'Yes, of course! … I remember that

night when he started on Jonathan. It's funny in retrospect, Jonathan should've shrugged it off.'

'It's no laughing matter … And, Greg was slagging him off for being a capitalist anyway.'

'I know. But instead of hearing it as an insult, Jonathan could've taken it as a compliment.'

'Dad!'

'When did he die?'

'Last week.'

'What a waste. I always thought his heart was in the right place,' Dad muses. 'You wouldn't ever do something like that, would ya?'

'No, of course not!' I snapped back.

On top of the table, two of the four beer mats are in use. Dad's pint on his beer mat. My pint only half on mine, I think of straightening it but instead pull the ashtray towards me and take out a gold packet of Benson & Hedges and a lighter.

'That's a disgusting habit. A slow suicide in a way.'

'I've cut down … I'm giving up.' I lit up and took a drag.

'Greg was a good man … for a Marxist,' states Dad in a matter-of-fact voice.

'He drowned in the Thames – the current pulled him under.' I take a longer drag and let out the smoke.

'Shit! … At least, not like one of those who jump in front of a train – so inconsiderate!'

'That's not funny!'

'No, definitely not to the commuters having to wait —'

'You don't always have to pretend to be a tough guy.'

'Fair enough.' He shrugged.

'Apparently, in his suicide note he wrote that since the Empire was reduced to a small rock in the South Atlantic, what's the point?'

'Talking of Greg's early doors, my round, can I get you another?' Dad points to my empty.

'Yeah, sure … I've room to stick it down my whatsit!'

Dad stands up straight. He has good posture for a man in his late-sixties. He stretches before picking up his cardboard box. He goes to stand at the long dark wooden bar, laid out along one side of the high-ceilinged White Lion.

Behind the bar is the Australian barman, with a scrawny neck, standing between the hand pumps, the till and a picture of the 1966 squad on the wall. He is having a heated conversation with an old guy, in an Adidas sweatshirt, sitting on a bar stool.

Dad motions to the barman; when the guy finishes whatever he had been arguing about, he saunters over to Dad.

I remain seated, tap out ash into the ashtray and draw down on my fag. The smoke doesn't cover the pub smells of old furniture and spilt beer. I consider how coming here has become a new routine for Dad and me, every Tuesday afternoon. It's a quiet time at work for me, I don't even change out of my white overalls or checked trousers. It's much the same each week – I tell myself I wouldn't tolerate his mockney if I didn't love him.

Good choice, UB40! I hum along: 'H hu-hu hu-hu hu hum hu hu.' I only stop when I hear the heartiest of laughs coming from two men two tables away. Ali Campbell had been singing: '… burden of shame.' I notice one of them is holding in one hand a bag with a squash racket sticking out. They seem to have halves of shandy. I assume a post-match drink and they aren't UB40 fans.

Dad brings his box of souvenirs back and puts it down on the floor again. He returns to the bar to collect a pint of Foster's for me, a pint of IPA for himself and a packet of peanuts to share. As he finally sits down right beside me, I can smell his Paco Rabanne. Alongside each other is the best, we watch the goings-on in the pub, not missing anything, and can look each other in the eye, if need be.

'We had a great Empire once, son. And, Britain used the East India Company to teach the Septics how to use business to further their aims.'

I looked around quickly to make sure no one else heard that. 'Are you still *trying* to be funny? It's not working.'

Dad leans forward and grins. 'How's Tina?'

'Tina?' I cross my arms across my chest. 'What about Tina? Yeah, I went to school with her. She's great … If it wasn't for Jono and the kids maybe, at one time, I'd have —'

Dad moved on, 'Your business?'

'Yeah good.' I uncross my arms. 'They love Modern English cuisine in Plaistow. I have enough corn to get me by … Can't grumble.'

'Tina's Jonathan's wife?'

I look to the ashtray and toss my cigarette butt in. 'Yeah, and Jono and I own the business. There isn't anything more to say really!'

We sup on our pints.

Two lads in shirtsleeves, officer workers out early, buy a pitcher of Bud; the barman laughs at something one of them says.

'I could have been a journalist, you know,' Dad says abruptly, 'I'm a natural.' Dad pulled at his ear. 'I've still got it. I was able to deduce what was going on between you two, easy enough … I couldn't be bothered with all the study needed. I made the right choice.'

My arms are back across my chest. 'Yes, Dad. You have told me before.'

'It was either journalism, astronaut or business, and I chose business. The money's good.'

'Paid for the education you keep telling me I've wasted.'

'We used to need the privately educated young men to run the colonies.'

'Don't be daft – I'm just a simple lad.'

'Simple is right. You and Tina in the Black Horse!' Dad tilts his head slightly towards me.

'So we're back on this again? Tina? Yeah, OK, I saw her yesterday in there. We were … It was just a coincidence we were both in there.'

'What about Jonathan? Where was he?'

'No, Jono was working.'

'Did he mind?'

'No, why would he mind?'

Dad gives me a look.

'I don't know what you think you are getting at but no, I would not! He's my mate, my business partner. Yes, she's attractive —'

A look of empathy crosses my dad's face. 'Son, I was once your age, I know how it is.'

'Now hold on —'

'Son, you were spotted, more than holding hands.'

I splutter on my pint and spray a little beer across the table. 'Sorry … What do you mean?' Dad is silent. 'Please don't say anything to Jono.' My legs start to shake up and down. Who bloody spotted me? Who told Dad? Shit, did they tell Jono? I force my legs to stop fidgeting. 'How do you know?'

'The old-fashioned way. I saw you. I was in there selling —'

'Thank God!'

'Son, mixing work and pleasure ...' Dad put his hands up to stress I was being an idiot. 'I was always told it's not a good idea.'

'Don't … It would break his heart if he found out Tina was cheating on him.'

'This is your work partner we are talking about! Is it worth it?' He puts extra stress into his question.

'Keep your voice down! You wouldn't —'

'It's not any of my business, son.'

'Good.'

'Does she have feelings for you?' Dad leans forward and tilts his head to show he is listening.

'It's not like that.'

Dad hums: 'What about you?'

'It's fun.'

'But if he loves her?' Dad seems earnest.

'They sleep in separate rooms. She says they hadn't had sex for —'

'Woah, son!'

'Well, to be honest, how could I resist, she's a corker. I offered a meal for two and she didn't say no.'

'I guess worse things happen at sea.'

'You're definitely not going to say anything?'

'It's been like this ever since the sexual revolution. That's something America brought us ... You've been caught with your hand in the cookie jar.'

I don't want to talk about this subject any more and dad seems to have had his say, so we drink quietly.

A minute later, I whisper: 'You wouldn't inform on me, would you?'

'No.'

'And I promise not to make any play for Tina again.'

'If she asks?'

'I don't know. I'd have to think about it. Does a gentleman turn down a lady?'

Dad hums. We drink.

I smell deep-fried food as the Australian barman walks past

with a plate of burger and chips in one hand and cutlery in the other. He puts them down on the squash player's table and points towards condiments at the end of the bar.

Dad speaks. 'Now, on every high street you can get a wide range of burgers and muffins. We can go to a drive-thru' for a nice iced donut. We even have a coffee named after our new master.'

'You're living in the past, Dad.'

'We've come a long way from the steak and kidney pie.'

If I'm not careful there's going to be a whole lot more cockney shtick. 'I like a steak and kidney pie.'

'Yeah so do I ... What I meant was we have come a long way from the time when we ruled. As we're now down to the Falklands, it's either go in with Europe or America. I don't like it. We need to get out of the EEC.'

'You mean the EU, Dad.'

'I don't want us ruled by anyone.'

'We aren't a big player anymore.'

'You're right there, son. We're the pipsqueak in the playground – lusting after US power. Got to get some of that sense of importance on their coat-tails. We follow them around like, what's the word ... poodle.'

I've heard this sort of thing many times before. Once I responded by saying I didn't really care; that didn't even stop Dad's flow. I try something new: 'You, Dad, seem to be proud to tell it as you see it. You know what that is? Pure American!'

'Fair play, for all my talk, I too have become American.'

'Do you feel guilty?'

Dad stifles a groan. 'A little I guess, but the money dampens the pain.'

'Isn't that a sell out?'

'Hunting the Greenback? Or Britain as a theme-park?'

'Either … both!'

'We deliver the Yanks historical monuments, Bronte Country and Jack the Ripper walks. We've Disneyfied ourselves and they pay us.'

'You get paid in pounds not dollars or euros … for the time being.'

'I don't mind as long as I'm paid.' He leans back with his hands behind his head.

I want another cigarette but suppress the urge. 'I know you made your biggest money from the Charles and Diana plates.'

'Mohamed Al Fayed says he's "99.9% certain" it was a conspiracy to kill Diana and Dodi.'

'You're not going to sell many of those Diana plates any more?'

'You'd be surprised.' Dad laughs.

Two tables away, the barman returns to deliver a long sausage in a crusty roll to the second squash player. After, the barman comes over to Dad and hands him £500.

Dad winks at me: 'A monkey!'

Dad doesn't half lay it on thick sometimes. He's a genuine cockney. Well, he says he is. 'What was that for? … You're meant to be retired.'

'A hundred T-shirts personalised for the pub plus one *vintage* Charles and Di plate.'

I laugh: 'They won't shift one hundred —'

'I've already delivered the right sizes for the bar staff, five-a-side football, darts (male and female) and chess teams.' Dad grins.

'How many is that?'

'Thirty.'

'Only seventy to go!'

'They're going behind the bar, starting price: a score … We're going to do the same in your and Tina's Black Horse and then – if all goes well – we can go across the whole pub chain … Could be a real nice earner!'

I ignore the little dig. 'Dad, don't you ever stop?'

'It keeps me going, son,' he grins.

'You don't have to, you know.'

'I know.' Dad sighs. After a little quiet, he adds, 'We chase the Yankee dollar but we still play football and darts.'

'Yeah, we haven't gone crazy for the American football just yet … I still love the Hammers.' Inadvertently, I look to the TV (off), high up in the corner. 'We're on fire at the moment!'

'You'll have to call it soccer in the future.'

'Ha! So, is that why you now like to be thought of as a tough guy rather than a hard man?'

'That's for others to decide.'

'Could you really have been an astronaut, Dad?'

115

Dad's eyebrows shot upwards. 'They didn't have that many opportunities in my day. Few astronauts and fewer popstars.'

'But you have a great voice, Dad.'

'To be fair, if I'd had an agent, perhaps, I could have been an opera singer.'

'As long as you don't let slip about the other matter, sing to your heart's content.'

'No, of course not, son.' Dad pauses – he looks as if he is contemplating something.

I can hear one of the squash players as he is talking loudly, over the clinking of glasses.

Dad says: 'I'm confused. If Greg was a Marxist shouldn't he have been happy the Empire was reduced to just the Falklands?'

The mention of Greg jolted me. 'Many, many things had gone wrong for Greg. No point analysing it, Dad. We'll never be able to get into his head to feel what he felt.'

'True.' Dad raises his glass, 'To Greg.'

I raise my glass, 'Greg.'

We drink deeply.

Dad stands up, 'Perhaps some music that I actually like this time.'

'Spice Girls?'

Dad pulls a face.

'Geri Halliwell in that Union Jack dress?'

Dad bobbles his head left and right as if considering what I have said then pulls his lips back and raises a palm as if saying: Not such a bad idea! He walks over to the jukebox.

On his return, his choice of music is playing: Who Do You Think You Are. He points to our empty glasses. 'Want another?'

I stand up. 'I better not.' I look at my watch. 'I've got to get back to *my spices*. See you next week, Dad.'

'There Is No Alternative,' he grins.

14. LIFE AFTER DEATH

The window gave Niall a panoramic view. In the distance he could make out modes of transport – a small train along its tracks, cars on the motorway, a plane in the air. Actual people, walkers and cyclists were also moving but they were too insignificant to show any detail.

There was the clink of ice on glass. He turned and examined her as she handed him one of two gin and tonics. She was just as he had ordered; shapely figure, pretty face, she even wore a Gucci leopard-print top.

She placed the second gin and tonic down on the glass coffee table that dominated his long, big-windowed living room. In its centre were the fresh red tulips his PA had ordered, in a cut-glass vase. His ex-wife had loved tulips. The woman showed no interest in the flowers. If her hair was a shade darker, she might look a bit like his ex.

The woman sat back in the expensive curved leather sofa beside her drink. She hadn't uttered a word since her arrival – that showed class.

Niall knew this was his time. His suit was sharp; he wore his shirt, without a tie, the top two buttons undone to project that he was ready for action. Hands on hips he broadcast: 'Every sated temptation is a new fund of self-knowledge.'

'"The only way to get rid of temptation is to yield to it," that was Oscar Wilde,' she said.

He could see something in her pretty face, perhaps admiration. She certainly was paying full attention, good girl. 'I like to take my time —'

'Sating desire or deciding your right from wrong?'

'You need time with desire ... There is no right and wrong until someone defines it.' As he spoke, she picked up her drink and sipped it. 'In today's world money is right. Where would we be without the wealth creators and entrepreneurs?' He left the question hanging as he took a glug from his drink. 'Probably no better than a third world nation ... People have told me I've been lucky.' He laughed. 'The lucky are the weak losers, born with a silver spoon, inherited wealth and don't they lord it over everyone else? No, I don't believe in luck. I had to pull myself up from the gutter – that's a real education ... Now, I know circumstances will come along, I am ready. I'm adaptable. Dynamic ... If more people thought like me this country could quickly be reborn.'

Niall took a brown envelope from his suit jacket's inside pocket. She smiled as he put the envelope down on the glass table in front of her.

'I give a lot of my money away.' Niall fiddled with a gold

cufflink. 'Last month, I was generous to Help for Heroes and the Police Memorial Trust. I make political donations too, to whoever promotes law and order. The current government are certainly not up to it … We can't have burglars, thieves or muggers prospering. I support whoever strengthens the laws to lock up the criminals.'

She picked up the envelope and put it in her large handbag; he could see the Mulberry label. As she closed the clasp, she spoke: 'Don't they say money makes the world go around?'

'Yup, unlike the born wealthy, I bring a huge amount to this country. OK, I pay my accountants to organise my wealth and my taxes, but I bloody well pay everything I'm meant to pay! I agree with the Guardianistas: Nobody is strong enough to deal with the scroungers who don't pay their fair share. Yes, lock up all the tax dodgers that break the law.'

'We must protect the new status quo, sir,' she said.

The doorbell rang.

Niall looked the woman up and down, not intending to answer the door.

The bell rang again.

'Are you going to answer that?' she asked.

'I wasn't going to, no.' He stood up and moved to the front door. He looked through a spyhole and then sighed as he opened the door.

A good-looking young man with tidy hair, in a suit and white shirt, was outside. He wore a black name badge which read: Elder Joshua Gardner. He was smiling and holding a dark brown Bible. 'I hope I'm not disturbing you —'

'How did you get into this building?'

'Every day, I create conversations about religion with strangers.'

'I asked you a simple question: How did you get in?'

'We came for Sunday lunch.'

'We?'

'Elder Lomey and I ... John Smee, on the ground floor, is my uncle. But Elder Lomey had a migraine. He is lying down now in the dark. I shouldn't have left him, I should be with my missionary companion 24 hours a day, but he isn't going anywhere.'

'Your mission isn't to be up here bothering me!'

'The second Mrs Smee told me the view is wonderful. Yes, selfishly I came up here and then I remembered the reason why we are all here. Today is Sunday, the Holy day.'

'Yes, SUN-day a pagan day for worshiping the Sun. And yes you are disturbing me. Please —'

'The Lord gave us the seventh day to rest. I'd like to ask if —'

'Pleeaase!'

'Have you ever considered life after death?'

'I've asked you nicely.'

The woman came to the door and stood beside Niall – the ice in her gin and tonic gently clinked against the glass in her hand. 'You boys need to lighten up. If you like ... I know just the right girls.'

Niall saw the grin on her face and couldn't resist the urge to laugh. 'Why don't you come on in.' He beckoned into his flat, with an open hand. 'Would you like a drink … Joshua?'

'A glass of water.'

'Nothing stronger?'

'No, water's fine.'

'You're an American, aren't you? Please sit down or enjoy the view out my window if you like.' They all sat on the long curved leather sofa. The woman sat between the two men. Niall continued: 'Mormon?'

'Yes. I received the mission call for sacred service.'

'So, you are a missionary?'

'I came to your door to teach and contact. Missionaries talk about faith, the gospel of Jesus Christ to bring converts to the faith.'

'Ever had a woman?'

Joshua reddened. 'No sir. I wait like all good … until I'm married.'

'Do you think this woman is pretty?' Niall signalled with his hand. He spotted Joshua's eyes move to the woman and then dart away.

Joshua didn't answer his question, he smiled faintly.

'You can have her now if you like. No questions asked. There is a choice of four bedrooms.' Niall pointed, 'the best is there … through that door.'

'No, sir. That's just not right. I am here to talk about God's plan for mankind that is happiness and redemption.'

Niall laughed loudly. 'What if I make it interesting and said I'd give you ten … no forty thousand pounds to sleep with her?

Surely you would be mad not too.'

'How can you say such a thing?'

'No one, except us three will ever know.' Niall rubbed his wrist, where the strap of his Rolex was tight. 'And once you leave, you'll never see either of us ever again.'

'No, it's wrong.'

'Doesn't she have a lovely pair of legs?'

'What you are saying – it's wrong.' Joshua stood up.

'That's just your mind speaking. What does your body say? "Yes" – I can hear it saying "Yes!" Just look at her. A magnificent creature!'

Niall took a wad of £50 notes from his inside jacket pocket and put it down on the table – it was held together with a strip that read: £2,000.

Joshua stared at the money before saying, 'My faith doesn't permit me to —'

Niall interrupted, 'Give all the money to your church if you like, I don't care.'

'I couldn't. It's —'

'Would you deny the charity of your choice all that could be bought for £40,000? That's your choice.' Niall caught the woman's eye and nodded. She stood up, straightened her skirt and approached Joshua.

'Stop, you mustn't come any closer.'

'What? Are you afraid of her?' laughed Niall.

'Please, I cannot be within an arm's length of you.' Joshua

was staring at the woman. 'All the problems between man and God stem from Adam and Eve going against God's wishes when they ate the fruit in the Garden of Eden.'

'What a load of baloney!' Niall laughed. He nodded to the woman as he addressed Joshua, 'Don't be an idiot and turn down this opportunity.'

She took Joshua's hand; he offered no resistance as she led him into the nearest bedroom.

'Leave the door open,' called out Niall as he made himself comfortable; he removed his black shiny slip-on shoes.

*

Half an hour later, Joshua sat beside the coffee table, with a forlorn look on his face. There was a £40,000 pile of cash in front of him. Niall had been to his safe, hidden behind an abstract line drawing by Paul Klee, in his second reception room.

Facing Joshua, on the other side of his coffee table, Niall was pleased with himself, he had correctly read human nature. He asked the woman to fix him another drink. She looked a little dishevelled.

'I feel dead inside,' said Joshua.

'Well, you'll soon know what life after death is like then and let me tell you, it's just fine.'

'Jesus Christ died on the cross to resolve the problems between humans and God. But, I am not Jesus, my heart is shrivelled … I feel dirty.'

'Wake up. That's just life.'

'You're an evil man. You're not going to be saved. And

neither am I now.'

'Go and get baptised again. Or confess. Or whatever you Mormons do.'

'It doesn't work like that.'

'You'll be fine. You're young. You have £40,000 in your pocket. The whole of your life is in front of you.'

'My life has ended.' Joshua's voice was flat and tired.

Niall laughed.

Suddenly, Joshua leapt at him. The vase of red tulips fell and both men ended up on the floor. Niall flailed with his arm and his watch collided with the coffee table. Joshua wrapped his hands around Niall's neck. He felt them squeeze and hit out with both his fists. His right hand hit Joshua in the face. Joshua increased the pressure on Niall's neck, he was pressing hard; Niall's face felt hot. Niall tried to speak but the sounds were choked.

Close by, the woman shouted: 'For God's sake, you'll kill him. Stop. Turn the other cheek!'

Joshua let go, sat down on the floor and started to cry.

Niall crawled away from Joshua, rubbing his neck. He lay down on the leather sofa and looked at the woman: 'Thank you.' A few seconds later, he added: 'Can you fix me a drink? … What's your name, by the way?'

'You can call me Gail.' She moved over to Joshua and put a hand on his shoulder. 'Would you like anything?'

He shook his head in the negative.

Gail picked up the unbroken vase and tulips and took them

into the kitchen. She shouted: 'You're all out of tonic!'

She returned to the living room and pulled on her coat.

Niall said to Joshua: 'You're not that religious after all, are you?' He checked his watch for damage, he could hear the sound of it ticking. It read: 2:25pm.

'You and I are of the earth,' said Joshua.

'What does that mean?'

'We are of this earth, not heavenly beings!' There was anger and shame in Joshua's voice.

'You held yourself in such high esteem you were bound to become one of the fallen,' said Niall.

'We are crass and sinful animals with animal passions,' sniffed Joshua.

'You know what they say, what goes up must come down.'

'Do you even try?'

'Try what?' asked Niall. 'Living? Being a moron?'

'Being a Mormon is life!'

'Come on, boys, please stop arguing. I'll make us fresh drinks.' Gail picked up her handbag. 'I'll be back in a minute.'

As she pulled the front door closed behind her, Niall said: 'You're such a faggot!'

Joshua with enlarged eyes and lips downturned, stared at Niall with an intense gaze. 'You've got loads of stuff but you've lost your soul.'

'Grow up! We're all commodities, Joshua.' Niall turned to pick up a glass from the table, he expected a drink to be waiting there. 'You think you're special, you're not!'

Controlling his anger, Joshua said: 'I'd like to go now.'

Niall didn't reply.

'Where is my £40,000?' asked Joshua.

Niall still didn't reply. There was no drink and no money and no Gail.

'I want that £40,000!' demanded Joshua. 'NOW!'

15. READY?

A light-green coloured truck stops outside an apartment building.

The driver, in a green shirt and white pants, steps from the truck. He opens the back doors and carries grocery bags over to the front door.

He presses the bell for number 16. There is no response. He presses number 16 again. Again, no response. He presses the button marked: Concierge.

The doors unlock with a buzz. The delivery man pushes the door open and sees inside that a man in a dark suit is waiting. The delivery man looks at a piece of paper and says: 'I've eight ready meals, bread, waffles, shaving foam, razor blades and toothpaste for a Mr Jabri Naifa, apartment 16.'

'Yes, I can take them,' says the man in the dark suit.

*

On Wednesday afternoon before dusk, Jabri sits in his favourite armchair holding a red cup. Late autumn sunlight pours through the open window warming his face.

In his Ray-Ban Aviator shades, white dress-shirt open at the collar, khaki pants, bare feet and Armani tie loose, he feels relaxed. He carefully loosens the tie further: *Syna bought me this tie as a birthday present. She was a beauty. The first time I saw her was in a bar in the Bronx; she was wearing cut-off jeans and a hoodie. She looked good in everything: silk blouse and skirt; pants suit and heels; or even, summer dress and trainers.*

He enjoys basking in the light, occasionally sipping at his coffee. *It has been eighteen months since we last ate together.* He considers going to the kitchen for a cinnamon cookie: *No, I'll eat supper soon enough.*

Jabri grips his hand around his cup. *My fingers are becoming bony. My flesh so thin.* He sets the cup aside beside a small brass Lord Vishnu statue, a present from his mother, on a small table next to him. He puts his hands in his pockets and keeps them there.

He continues to sit in the armchair as the day darkens but now he can't seem to get comfortable. He is restless and shifts in his seat. *There's an ache in my left buttock. Could it be something serious? Maybe just a muscle knot? I'm worrying more nowadays.* The passing of day into evening is less pleasant. *I can't figure it out. What is bothering me? Maybe it's living alone? Maybe I still miss Syna?*

She doesn't want anything to do with me now. There was always an age difference. Her last contact was a scribble on a cheap postcard from Thousand Islands: Great you got the place – enjoy the apartment warming. S x. Jabri takes a deep breath and lets it out slowly. His heart beats evenly as he remembers the end of an early date: *We were sitting on a bench in Central Park when I told her she was 'special'. I watched her bend her head around to look at me as if for the first time. She said: 'You're special to me too, Jabri.' I felt so happy. I tried to keep a straight face but couldn't. It was funny how our declarations came out. We both laughed.*

A breeze rustles the curtains. The sun is falling. It is getting too dark and Jabri stands up. Underfoot, the polished wooden floor is warm from the sun. He looks to the picture of his late Father and Mother on the wall. *Father taught me: 'Within seven seconds of meeting someone, they will make their impression of who you are. You never get a second chance to make a great first impression.'* He straightens his tie and picks up the cup. The last bit of sun turns the cup's red colour almost orange. He finishes his coffee in one.

Going to the kitchen, his feet make a soft sound on the wooden floor. He puts the cup in the sink. A single upside-down glass tumbler sits on the draining board. To calm himself, he picks it up, fills it with tap water and takes a sip. It is cool and reassuring going down his throat.

He saunters back to the living room to catch the dying of the late sunlight. He stands beside the window holding the tumbler in his left hand, takes his sunglasses off and rubs his eyes with his right.

I feel shivers. Both hands begin to shake violently. The tumbler falls to the ground and smashes. There is something to the side of him in the room. Its sudden appearance scares him. He does not know what it is. The apartment is empty. He turns. *I see a dark shape. A visitor to my apartment? Don't be stupid, keep calm, move away. It's probably nothing.* But he doesn't move away. In reflex, he reaches out his hand into the darkness. *I stretch towards the wall … whatever it is, it is on the stone and it feels cold.*

Jabri hears a groaning sound. He withdraws his hand and the dark shape vanishes.

Reaching out to touch the darkness wasn't sensible. It was no shadow. The visitor is alive, moving, but cold. Jabri's heart seems to have stopped, his mouth is dry and his palms clammy. *Its movements are different from mine. The dark shape is separate. A ghost? If it had a face, it would be serious with a determined expression. If it spoke it might say: 'I know what I want and I will calmly and resolutely never stop until it is achieved.'* A wave of anxiety engulfs Jabri. *My head is full of the sickness, pain and suffering.*

Jabri has cramps in his guts as if he might lose control of his bowels. *Am I touching death? Is my time up? Have I done enough for a happy afterlife? I have so much I want to do. I'm too young. Calm down! These are feelings – I'm alive.*

Jabri feels a little better. *Perhaps I'm stressed. Perhaps I'm mistaken and it was nothing more than shadows in the changing of the light?* He looks around his living room; at first, he takes nothing in. There is water and broken glass near his feet; he imagines walking on a razor-sharp sliver that would pierce the skin of his foot with ease. He can hear his heartbeat in his ears. *If it was something, could it stalk me? Silently follow me?* That thought unnerves him. Scares him.

He scans the room: *The television looks normal.* The two armchairs – one for the window, one for the TV – are unchanged, the cushions of the one facing the window still dented by his shape. Each chair with its own side table. And, in the corner, his desk with computer, printer, chair and trash can. *Normal too.*

Night is coming. Shadows move on the walls as the daylight fades. *It's getting dark. I need to put on the lights.* Jabri presses the living room light switch, but nothing happens. He tries again – it still doesn't come on.

He tries a table light. *No! Nothing is working!*

Jabri goes into his kitchen for a roll of paper towel and a dustpan and brush. He tries the light switch there. Nothing. *Everything is against me!*

It is getting darker back in the living room. He places the biggest pieces of glass very carefully in the dustpan. He soaks up the water with three paper towels. He sweeps smaller glass shards into the dustpan. *It's too dark for this.* Trying to pick up one of the final splinters he nips himself. *Fuck!* He wraps the finger in a fresh paper towel. He takes everything back to the kitchen. He tries the light switch again. No light comes on. *But there is something else – a presence in the kitchen.* It groans – it is a helpless groan. *I see the dark shape again.* Jabri can feel panic returning as the visitor becomes clearer. *It wears only black. Black the colour of the weary.*

He can now see the visitor does have a face, discoloured to grey. In the gaunt cheeks, Jabri finds so much of his own face – it is serious and determined. *I feel the cold touch of my disapproving ancestors.* And then he recognises his mother's face – as she was when she tore the dead heads off wilted flowers. *I should have flown to her as soon as I heard she was ill. I could have supported her. Is this her ghost wanting to say goodbye?*

Jabri hears a disconnected voice from the vicinity of the dark shape: 'You can't ever divide blood.' *It doesn't sound like Mother.*

Jabri replies: 'I hear you ...' *This thing, whatever it is, didn't do me any physical harm earlier but it seems to be closer to me. Why can I see more of it now?* '... What do you want?'

'How are you?' asks the voice.

'Busy ... as ever.' Jabri can see the microwave clock. It reads 20:36; its electricity is working. *Perhaps the fridge was working too. The fridge has a light.* He opens the fridge: *No light!*

Ready meals fill the top shelf. They are still cold to the touch. He takes out a meal for two.

'Pray to the Lord, son.'

Could it be?

'Yeah. Sure.' Jabri lays the table for two, clattering knives and forks on purpose; it makes the situation feel a bit more normal.

'Will you be ready, Jabri?'

'I hope so, but that's hard to tell, nobody judges themselves.' *Have I done enough with my life? Father was a doctor, he saved lives. We could have made life: if Syna hadn't had that miscarriage our child would be almost three.*

'Pray for His forgiveness for past sins!' says the voice. It is louder this time. *That's the sort of thing she'd say after temple.*

'Of course!' Jabri sets the timer on the microwave then takes a sharp knife from a drawer and uses it to stab five times at the plastic film lid of the ready meal. He likes the 'pop' sounds it makes. *Maybe I have pent-up anger?*

'In following His path, you will find peace,' says the voice.

'I bought this chicken curry from the Stop and Shop. It's good. I've had it before.' Jabri places the ready meal into the microwave, shuts the door and presses the start button. The machine gives off a reassuring hum as the food rotates.

'In following His path, you can find contentment ... Are you ready?'

The sound of the microwave pinging followed directly on from the disconcerted voice.

'It's nearly ready ...' Jabra takes the meal out and pulls back the plastic film lid from the two compartments. He stirs rice then stirs chicken curry. Returning the meal to the microwave, he resets the timer and presses start again. The machine's reassuring hum returns.

The visitor groans. It is a pained noise like disapproval of the appliance humming.

'It was just like how I remembered a curry should be,' Jabri says. 'Yellow chilli paste, with big cut onions. It is absolutely marvellous.' Behind him, he hears the scraping of a chair across the kitchen floor.

'In time, Jabri. God willing, you shall have a healthy ...'

End.

16. FLAT BREAD

When I return from work, there is still a faint smell of fresh paint. The living room walls were painted yellow that morning. The landlord must love primary colours; the sagging sofas are red and blue.

I sit down on the blue sofa with my *Evening Standard*. Five and then ten minutes later, respectively, Pete and Suzie join me in the living room.

I read in the quiet atmosphere: *The congestion in London today was 'unacceptable', says the city's top transport official. Transport Commissioner Alex Thomson called it a 'once in a lifetime event' and admitted TfL had no contingency plan.*

Suzie sighs; clearly audible for all of us to hear.

Looking up, I catch her eyes. She is lying on the red sofa; short, plump and smartly dressed. She is always smartly dressed, even before going to bed. She likes to wear the colours of nature – browns and greens. Maybe she loves secondary colours?

I hold her stare to communicate annoyance at being

disturbed. A TV listings magazine is open on the occasional table beside her. Her handbag on the floor. Between us, there are dust particles suspended in the air, illuminated in the light coming through the window. I only break my stare to return to the article: *The traffic in the vicinity was messed up all morning, as Transport for London worked tirelessly to remove the unexpected guests to the Strand underpass.*

There is another sigh followed by movement on my left. I turn my head to look at Pete. He is sitting beside me, all in black, on the blue sofa. He only ever wears black clothes except for his red dressing gown. He is looking at Suzie, with bemused eyes; he picks up then digs his right hand, with its Celtic cross tattoo, into a blue family-sized packet of salt and vinegar crisps; he puts one crisp into his mouth and pauses, keeping his fingers on the edge of his mouth. He chews with his mouth open probably on purpose: 'Crunch, crunch, crunch.'

I go back to my *Evening Standard*:

… guests to the Strand underpass. The red transit van skidded on a slushy mixture of ice and sand. The load of bread was shed across ….

'Th … ohh!' moans Suzie.

'What is it?' says Pete.

'Nothing,' says Suzie.

Pete stands up and mumbles: 'If I wanted drama I'd go to the theatre.' He departs to the kitchen with its yellow cupboards, red chair and sky-blue fridge, leaving Suzie with me and my *Evening Standard*.

…. shed across the entrance to the underpass running from Waterloo Bridge to the Kingsway. The van turned on its side discharging bagels ….

Suzie addresses me: 'David, David, do you like Pete?'

.... baguettes, Mother's Pride, bread ....

'David!'

'What?' I put my newspaper down into my lap.

'Do you actually like Pete?'

'Yeah, why?'

'It`s just ... you know?'

'No.'

Suzie takes a white and green packet of menthol cigarettes from her handbag. 'After I said we have different definitions of *clean* ...' From the full length of her arm, she holds an unlit cigarette delicately dangling between two fingers of her right hand. 'You know, he`s been so unfriendly.'

'He isn`t to me.'

'Oh.' Suzie stands up over the small table.

In the quiet, I pick up where I had left off reading my newspaper.

..... baguettes, Mother`s Pride, bread rolls out of its back. They cascaded over the bridge and into the mouth of the tunnel. The tunnel had to be closed. The traffic in Aldwych and the surrounding areas were slowed for the next two hours ...

'Th ... ohh!'

... as birds swarmed towards the underpass. At the entrance, pigeons and sparrows congregated to peck away at the discarded bread. Unfortunately for London drivers ...

Suzie is still standing – I can feel her presence. I try to zone her out so I can read.

... many of the birds made their way into the tunnel that by-passes

Aldwych in ....

Suzie moans loudly: 'Ohh!'

'WHAT is it?' I purposefully scrunch up the newspaper into a ball of blacks, whites and red.

'You don`t have to be like that.'

'Please I'm trying to read …'

'I know you all hate me in this flat.'

I slow my breath to deepen it. I put on a deadpan voice: 'Yeah that`s right – we all hate you.'

Suzie bursts into tears.

Egh! I've hurt her feelings – I didn't have to do that. I don't like seeing a woman cry.

There is pink in her cheeks to go along with minimal eye swelling.

Regret is a funny thing; they say it is worse not to do what you want to do than doing the wrong thing; but I don't know … I do know, I want to undo what I had just said but that is impossible. So, I try to placate her: 'We don`t hate you Sue, that was a joke, a bad joke. I was saying it for effect. Please don`t cry.'

She burbles: 'You do hate me – you all hate me.'

I pick up my red-top newspaper. And copying Pete, I go to the kitchen.

....in search of food.

17. NO TOAST

The letterbox clanked, when the letter arrived. I immediately recognised Jasper's handwriting when I picked it up from the doormat. I hadn't seen him for two days.

The telephone rang: 'Brring-brring!' The telephone has such an aggressive manner, doesn't it? I *can't cope with this!* I chucked Jasper's letter on the hall table, went into the kitchen and stared at the phone. *What am I going to do?*

Maddy shouted 'Mummy, Mummy the phone!' I sat down at the kitchen table and let it ring for a couple more times. *If it's important it'll go to the answer machine.*

'Mummy, it could be Daddy!' Maddy in her most flowery dress appeared at the kitchen door. She's always been a daddy's girl.

I mustn't break down in front of the children. If I can hold it together we will cope. 'I don't think so, dear.'

The ringing stopped and Maddy disappeared. I checked the phone: No message. Number withheld.

Maddy returned holding the letter out to me. 'Who's this

from?'

She's at the age when she wants to know everything. 'Thank you, dear.' I stuffed the letter in my handbag.

I picked up the phone and rang Nana's number. It rang, rang, rang with no answer. I left a message on her answer machine. 'Hi. It's Sara, your daughter.' As soon as I said this I realized how silly it sounded. Of course, she recognises the sound of her own daughter's voice. 'I need a favour. Will you babysit? … The toaster's broken and … I can go to Robert Dyas. Anyway, when you get this, can you call me back?'

As soon as I put the receiver down, the phone rang again with its sharp incessant rings: 'Brring-brring!' It had lost none of its malevolence. *Do I answer?*

Maddy shouted: 'Mummy … the phone!'

I picked up. It was Nana ringing back. I closed the door to explain about Jasper. She didn't understand but at least she was sympathetic. I asked: 'Can you babysit?'

'Of course, dear.'

'Great, you're a life saver. The toaster bust this morning …'

'What happened?'

'I was too vigorous trying to extract a —'

'You were always breaking things.'

'I know, I shouldn't —'

'So, what did the children eat?'

'Maddy had Weetabix, James Frosties. I —'

'They aren't healthy, so full of sugar —'

'I know you've got diabetes. What else could I —'

'Ever heard of proper food?'

'I wanted to do toast but the toaster was broke.'

'When you were a girl I was always able to —'

'OK … OK.' *She shouldn't tell me off. What else could I have done!*

'How long will you be?'

'See you in 45 to an hour.'

I rounded the kids up and made sure they were dressed warmly. James in an anorak over his jumper. A red duffle coat over Maddy's pretty flowered frock. Maddy whined, as she stroked the cat: 'Can Rusty come too?'

The cat with big eyes looked at me as if I had done something wrong.

'No!' I was a bit too sharp. To cover my mistake, I shouted to them both: 'Come on!'

There was something on the TV about the Queen and Theresa May. 'Turn it off, James.' I hadn't meant to shout, he looked so sweet squinting through his blonde hair. He only then said: 'I need the loo.' *That fringe needs cutting.*

As we waited for him to do his business, I checked for my keys, purse and Oyster card. Yes, all in my bag – with that bloody letter. The cat brushed herself against the leg of my black velvet trousers. I had to push her away.

All ready we made our way out, I double-locked the front door and we were off.

The underground was packed and no one would give up their

seat for the kids. Pretty normal. A man stood beside me wearing loafers, but the back of them were furry like slippers. I couldn't keep my eyes off them; Jasper keeps his loafers and his slippers under the bed. I had to tell myself to look away. *I'm not going to break down on the tube.*

Down the carriage, I saw three moving message boards – *how many do you need!* They all said in yellow dots: 'The next station is High Street Kensington. This is a District Line train to Edgware Road.' The last sentence changed as we approached the station: 'The next station is High Street Kensington. Mind the gap.'

A female voice repeated the exact same message over a Tannoy. James mimicked: 'Mind the GAP.' James and Maddy giggled. It was irritating.

The letter was the real cause of my irritation; I felt an uncomfortable desire to find out there and then what was happening. *I had to know!* Tears began filling my eyes until I remembered where I was. The train doors opened, I rubbed my face and called the kids to me so we could get off.

We exited the station, the children holding my hands. The high street was packed; office workers, woman shoppers and tourists. At least it wasn't far to Nana's. On arrival, neither of us were in the mood for small talk, a welcome escape.

After I had safely delivered the kids, I walked towards Robert Dyas. *If I can only keep on doing all the practical things we will be able to get through this.*

The woman shoppers all seemed to be wearing designer

clothes and heading in the same direction, towards what was Biba in the early '70s; but today, they will go down a set of stairs, in search of M&S food. I regarded two of the women greet each other with a 'darling' in plum voices and air kisses. They reminded me of the horsey set I went to school with.

I stopped off at the glass-fronted Caffè Nero beside Boots. *Mid-morning, it shouldn't be busy.* At the blue and black counter, I queued. I put my hand into my handbag for my purse and felt the letter. *No, not yet.* On reaching the front I ordered: 'A latte and two slices of brown toast, please.'

The waitress said. 'We don't do toast.'

'Oh!'

'Would you like a pastry with your grande coffee?'

She's trying to nudge me to spend more. In irritation, I said: 'No … No pastry and a regular, single shot, latte.'

'We do toasted sandwiches …'

'No … thanks.'

'No worries.'

I carried my latte, in its glass on a saucer, as I went in search of a comfortable chair. I knew upstairs would be quieter – the yummy mummies can't get their prams up the stairs.

I was lucky to find an unoccupied leather armchair at a small marble-topped table, where on the other side was a man in a dark suit reading a newspaper. Before sitting down, I cleared away debris, left by the previous customer, from my side of the table. I stayed away from the man's black coffee and croissant.

I made myself comfortable and reached out to feel the temperature of my latte – still too hot to drink. The man supped at his coffee as he read. When he ate his croissant, he leant in and I noticed he wore a colourful waistcoat. *Jasper has three colourful waistcoats.*

On opening my handbag, I caught a waft of my own cologne; I didn't have to rummage long to pull out the letter. I looked at his handwriting: *Well, here we go.* I ripped open the envelope. The sheet of paper in my fingers was the whitest I'd ever seen. I scanned it quickly first and choked up.

I looked away from the letter and dabbed at my eyes with a handkerchief to calm myself. *I mustn't break down.* I saw and brushed brown hairs off my velvet trousers. *Bloody cat.*

There were only a few people upstairs in Caffè Nero with me. The man opposite sat behind his copy of *The Times.* I was pleased I felt relatively anonymous in this public space.

When I felt near composure, I went back to the letter. There were still tears in my eyes as I read slowly: 'I had to keep telling you about the demands of my job. The kids will be better off without our constant fighting. You never understood me as Robin does.' I could feel my body shake. *It's so unfair. He didn't need to shag someone behind my back. Jasper needs to grow up, he's so selfish, he only thought of himself when he decided on the affair. There's no excuse for abandoning the children.*

I picked up my latte in both hands and drank comforting, hot and creamy foam. I put my coffee glass down in its saucer. *I'll go straight to Robert Dyas after here – it really should be the man's job to go to the hardware shop.*

I returned to Jasper's letter: 'I don't feel remorse; neither of us were happy. We could never be happy together.' I could feel anger rising: *He tries to shift blame; it's his fault – it's his shitty behaviour; but he blames us! What a pig! He's always been good at switching off feelings of guilt. He deceived me!*

I took my time to compose myself. *Well, bugger him. We are finished, defunct, dead.* I said out aloud: 'Jasper is toast!'

The man at my table looked over his newspaper and at me. I think he expected me to say something else. I smiled at him. *Probably thinks I'm mad.* He returned to his paper. *That waistcoat reminds me of bloody Jaspar.*

I'll move on: perhaps I will meet a better man? A new relationship? … I'll need to keep my focus on the children – no choice! … Jesus, what am I going to say to the kids?

I stood up. *Focus on the practical things. First on to Robert Dyas for that purchase. There will be toast and jam and orange juice for the kids' breakfast tomorrow.*

18. BREAKFAST WITH SONIA

Jack held Sonia by the arm as they walked down the high street. Jack carried a copy of the *Sunday People* in the back pocket of his blue jeans. They stopped outside the window of the jewellers and looked in. There were many sparkly trinkets: diamond earrings, silver loops, engagement rings, signet rings, gold studs, chain-link silver bracelets and fancy golden necklaces.

'What do you like the look of?,' asked Jack.

Sonia pointed. 'Oh, that's beautiful! Diamond and sapphire engagement ring *only* £2,995.'

'Anything you like can be yours.'

'You are ever so forward,' giggled Sonia.

They both laughed.

'Come on, let's get some grub in Tony's. I'm starving,' said Jack.

They strolled into the café next door. Pictures of EastEnders' stars were hung up on the wood-panelled walls.

Jack ignored the hustle and bustle at the front and headed for the relative calm of a booth of faux red leather at the side. Being more or less invisible was a blessing. Sonia followed.

Jack sat down knowing he could gaze on Sonia and still glance out the front window, to see the entrance to the jewellers and all the coming and going on the pavement outside.

Sonia was a picture. She wore green and purple that didn't match, but it didn't matter. Her beauty reflected out of her life experience. Dishevelled grey hair and twinkly eyes – a winning combination.

On the Formica table, in front of them, were two sets of cutlery each wrapped in a dark-green paper serviette. To the side was a laminated menu propped up between a cruet set, a glass sugar pourer and a bottle of Sarson's malt vinegar.

Jack put his *Sunday People* to one side of the table, beside the sugar, and picked up the menu.

'This place was in *Saga magazine*'s Top 10 Greasy Spoons,' said Sonia.

Jack looked over his menu. 'Really?'

'No, of course not. But it has a personal recommendation from Gillian Tayforth.' She nodded towards the Eastenders' pictures.

'Oh, this should be good then! She went up in my estimation after her fellatio performance.'

'Didn't they call it a pancreatic rub?'

'What goes on in a Chelsea tractor – stays in a Chelsea tractor.' He put the menu down.

'Oh, I hate those cars.' She picked the menu up.

'And I hate Chelsea,' Jack gurned; he had just reminded himself that on Saturday they had beaten Spurs at the Lane.

After a few minutes, a young Greek girl came over to take their order.

With her nose still in the menu, Sonia said, 'I'll have eggs, mushrooms, tomato, beans and chips. And can I have some ketchup for my chips?'

'I'll have the same with extra bacon, sausage and black pudding. And mustard for the side.'

Sonia looking up. 'Good idea. Can I have a sausage with mine too.'

'I thought you were vegetarian.'

'No.' Sonia added in a mock whisper: 'I would have thought you would have realised I eat meat after last night.'

Jack blushed and there was an awkward silence. The waitress, looking put out, asked, 'Tea or coffee?'

Sonia spoke sweetly, as if she hadn't said anything of consequence beforehand: 'A latte for me.'

'And a tea,' said Jack.

The waitress turned and walked away.

Smiling, Sonia looked Jack directly in the face. 'Do you remember, you tempted me with "How about a coffee?" last night.'

'I don't know what you mean.'

'And I'm still waiting … I had to order that one for myself.'

He grinned inanely. She really is lovely. Jack changed his expression, 'I DID give it to you though!'

'NOT the coffee that you promised ...'

Jack was still smiling when he said: 'I need the little boys' room.'

'You're not so little.'

Jack stood up. 'Thanks.'

Sonia picked up Jack's *Sunday People*. Yesterday's front page headline read: Silver Surfer Stealing Shopping Spree.

Jack heard her suppress her laughter. He was going to comment; he had already read the newspaper report on the old age pensioner crime wave sweeping the Home Counties: *They had used a computer to source the goods. Once a shop was targeted, a two-person (one man, one woman) hit-team was dispatched to do the actual stealing. The computer was again used to sell the contraband on eBay. Five people, all over 70, were helping the police with their inquiries but the police suspect there are still units operational. They stressed there was no danger or cause for the public to become alarmed.* His bladder wasn't what it was in his youth – Jack headed to the toilet.

After doing his business and returning to the table, Jack saw the latte and tea had been delivered.

Sonia looked up from the paper: 'Is that a canoe in your trousers or are you just pleased to see me?'

He gave her his lewdest grin. 'More like a space shuttle. There's always time for a re-entry.' He winked.

'Yeah? You need grounding!'

Jack put his hands in the air and shook them about. 'Oh no. Houston we have a problem!'

The banter came to a halt as the waitress placed two large plates in front of them and departed. Shortly afterwards she returned with a plateful of buttered white bread, and bright red and yellow plastic bottles.

Sonia said to the waitress: 'Oh, and can I have a glass of orange juice too.'

'Would you like ice with that?'

Sonia nodded. 'Yes.' She squeezed ketchup onto the side of her plate.

Jack shook salt and then squeezed ketchup all over his chips. Once this task was completed, he moved to the yellow bottle and squeezed out a large dollop of mustard beside his sausage, at the same time Sonia said: 'OJ will be the yin to all this greasy yang of a breakfast!'

'Yeah, you're having a well-balanced meal there!' He pointed with his knife, 'By adding orange juice to your mushrooms, tomato, beans and potato – that'll be your five-a-day done.'

Jack picked up the salt again to sprinkle generously onto the yellows of his eggs. He mixed it in using a long chip, before tucking into his chips using the yolk as a sauce.

'That lot will give you another heart attack,' said Sonia.

'Okay, I'll leave the beans.'

'Don't joke. I don't want to be left on my own.'

'Charming, just thinking about yourself!' He put a large piece of black pudding in his mouth and chewed.

'If you carry on like that, you'll be a drain on the NHS. Ever thought about going on a diet?'

'Look, I'll join Weight Watchers when you give up the fags … deal?'

'But what would I do after intercourse if I couldn't smoke?'

'Go to sleep?'

'That's the prerogative of the retired.'

The hubbub of voices in the café carried on around them as they ate without talking to each other.

Having nearly finished his breakfast, Jack said, 'After all this …' he made a circular movement with his fork over his plate, '… we should get back to work. I want to make the most of it while it lasts.'

'What?'

'Us as a team. Surfing for silver won't happen all by itself.'

'Okay …' She began drinking her latte with a teaspoon.

Jack leant in, conspiratorially, 'The jewellers is open. Five minutes ago, a young couple went in. After they've come out and as long as no one else goes in, we strike.'

'You know the drill. I try on the ring, you make a diversion and that's when I walk, yeah?'

'Yeah. I'm going to pretend to have a heart attack, don't be alarmed, nothing to do with this breakfast … just get out and go.' He wiped his empty plate with a piece of white buttered bread, leant his head back and added: 'You know, if you smoke after sex … maybe we're doing it a little bit too fast!'

19. MESMERISING

The door has just closed behind me and I sit in my chambers. It has been unique and I suspect I shall never experience its like again. I don't know how my peers will judge my reasoned conclusion in this case. I have carried out my task – to make all my comments based on my knowledge of the law – to the best of my abilities. I await the arrival of my assistant with the Braille transcript and later the jury's decision.

We were all told we had been chosen specially as the accused was 'mesmerising'. The jury is made up of twelve ordinary women chosen at random, from diverse backgrounds, religions and ethnic communities. I had insisted the jury was kept behind a fabric screen at all times, to ensure the lawyers would not be tempted to use hand signals or any other silent demonstrations. Each of the women took an oath to 'give a true verdict according to the evidence'.

I'm the judge because I am blind. I could never see the accused. Apparently, everyone, whether they know it or not, harbours implicit biases. In the criminal justice system this can really matter.

Lady Justice is often depicted blindfolded, as with sight comes bias. I was especially chosen because there would therefore be no visual stimulus that could trigger any of my biases related to beauty or race.

I first knew something was wrong with my vision when it became blurred at fifteen. My optician referred me to the hospital. A specialist there asked me how many fingers he was holding up; it was not absolute darkness, I could see a shape directly in front of me but nothing in peripheral vision. The specialist said my optic nerves were swollen and my treatment was steroids; they were of no use. I was informed the underlying cause was 'idiopathic', a word I had never heard before, but it told me the doctors also didn't know why the blindness had happened to me.

Loss of sight is a hideous experience. Over the next five months, I was nervous to leave the house. I had little social life and felt terribly isolated.

We live in a decent society. Most people are kind and considerate. I'm offered a hand by a stranger to help me cross a road. Yes, sometimes people forget they can just speak to me. It can be very helpful to hear 'move left', 'right' or 'stop'.

And there was help. Receiving a guide dog was a blessing, we clicked immediately. The dog changed my life. He gave me confidence. The range of things I felt able to do greatly widened. My dog obeys my orders and can recognise obstacles. I am lucky. Having a dog, instead of moving around with a cane, allows so much more freedom.

Over the years, I have adapted. Blindness did not stop me

studying the law. Then the RNIB were great at helping me get into a career, to apply it. Sir John Fielding, the Blind Beak of Bow Street, was my role model. Wanting to give something back was why I worked so hard to become a judge. The court house is a well-organised space. I've learnt to function here with minimal aid.

There is a knock on the door. My guide dog got to his feet. I say 'Enter.' It is my transcript. The jury have not yet come to their decision. I put the transcript into my 'to read tray', there must be no clutter in my private space. A tidy office is more pleasant and easier to navigate. Loose wires and bins are trip hazards.

The accused had been remanded in custody, deemed too dangerous for bail. As the judge, I set out the unusual court rules, for everyone's safety: The male bailiff and prosecution were blindfolded. The accused was made to wear both ankle and hand cuffs.

At the start of the trial, a number of women were called to the stand to give evidence, I didn't know if I should believe what I heard about the accused: 'She is a most beautiful woman with jet-black hair, scarlet lips and flame behind her eyes.' The first witness called her 'poisonous. This isn't a woman – it's a creature.' The second christened her the 'snake woman'. A third said: 'She is more cat-like than human.'

The female defence said: 'They are simply jealous of the body she displays in her tight-fitting dress …' This was the first time I realized she was dressed sexily – I had been led to believe people usually dressed soberly in court. The defence added: 'Or maybe these women's dislike comes from somewhere deeper.'

Bernard Turner, the owner of a chain of petrol stations, was called to the stand by the prosecution. He said: 'She is as attractive as siren song.'

The defence sought clarification.

'Men find it impossible to dislike her even after she has tried to kill them. Even after … I still visit her inside, bearing gifts,' said Mr Turner.

The defence counsel remained quiet; they had not contested that she knifed Mr Turner just because he told her he fancied her. They had called it 'provoked'.

The prosecution pointed out with a somewhat sarcastic tone: 'The opinions of the men, when she was successful, will never be known.'

The defence asked for the court to be cleared. The jury stood down for forty minutes of legal argument. The defence wanted the prosecution to withdraw the supposition of guilt implied by the word 'successful'. Eventually, the prosecution agreed to withdraw the word.

The accused was called to the stand. My guide dog got to his feet and began to growl. The accused hissed in our direction. I put my hand under my chair to calm him. My dog responded to my touch and lay down at my feet again.

Blindness had not diminished my sense of smell, quite the opposite. As she gave an oath of honesty, she was not too far away for me to know she exuded an alluring perfume.

The prosecutor asked questions and she talked to the court

about herself and the events, intelligently. Her accent was southern, posh and with a pleasant lilt. Listening to her, I didn't feel like anyone was in any danger; far from it.

I can vouch for her irresistible attraction being more than the purely physical, sexual or visual. She was clearly affecting me – it was a strong pull – she got under my skin. My mind was being captivated by something bewitching.

On remembering what had happened to Bernard Turner, I called for a change in the courtroom. There was a pause in proceedings to bring in electric fans and a sound system. I needed to ensure smells were dissipated and there was background white noise played across her words.

In her defence, she told the court: 'My kind are misunderstood.'

I had agreed that the final witness, Mr Hunter, could give his evidence from a separate room, as he requested for his protection. I listened to him being called to a stand, asked to place his hand on the Bible and then swear to tell the truth, the whole truth and nothing but the truth. He told the court: 'I had been warned to expect her and I was waiting in the shadows at the front of the shooting lodge, downwind as she has a heightened power of smell. Men had gone missing – she was our prime suspect.

'She drove up to the entrance in a red convertible Jaguar. When she stepped out of the car, her tight-fitting yellow and black striped silk dress and shiny brown skin showed off a taut body, much like the jaguar the car was named after. I put my nose in the air to try to read her scent. I have stalked in long grass; I know stripes blend with the grass. She avoided the grass, handed the keys to the attendant and headed inside toward the dining hall.

'I had wanted to make sure I and my colleague were there first. There was a Victorian wood and wire bird cage with a pair of love birds, a budgerigar and a canary, in a back room of the lodge. My colleague and I had discussed for over half-an-hour where best to put the birdcage. We put it in exactly the right place. She took her time in the corridor, distracted by the birds and my colleague and I were able to reach the dining hall before her.

'Eleven men were seated around a large rectangular table leaving one empty seat at the far end, beside Mr Turner. Her golden eyes darted to the trays of roast antelope, being brought to the long table set for a feast. Following the trays of antelope were vegetables hidden by silver cloches, she did not give the cloches of vegetables a second look. She moved stealthily towards the space left for her and sat down to eat with the men. Unknown to her, as she ripped into meat with sharp white teeth, I stalked her. I tugged a torch from my bag. I knew I almost had her. My colleague turned out the lights. And I shone the bright beam directly into her eyes. She was confused. She was trapped from going backwards by a Regency chair. She went left. Mr Turner was leaning in towards her, to kiss her, while my colleague stood in wait. She stabbed Mr Turner before she went right … and into my net.'

Many questions from the prosecution and defence followed. Mr Hunter's answers reiterated much of what he had already stated.

By the sixth day, we had heard both sides of the case. I reached and expressed my reasoned conclusion. I then sent the jury out to deliberate, telling them: 'Your decision on the outcome of the case must be based on your own judgements, no one else's.'

There was a second knock on my door. I was called to return to the courtroom. It had taken the jury three hours to come to their decision. The accused was found guilty of the attempted murder of Mr Turner. The jury's decision was unanimous.

At sentencing, I asked myself: Where do you put such a person? I considered showing leniency citing mitigating circumstances. After all, as I had noticed in the transcript, Bernard Turner admitted: 'You really shouldn't make a pass at a girl holding a knife at dinnertime.' I never got to make my sentence.

I heard screams and chomping as she devoured the jury. My dog was killed protecting me. Only when I heard sirens screeching in the distance did her presence leave the courtroom. At the same time as knowing I was saved, her leaving felt like a loss. I only survived through the loyalty of my dog and luck.

An investigation was ordered. How could I have got the situation so wrong? She had mesmerised a female bailiff officer to undo her cuffs and let her free. How could I have been blinded by my heterosexuality not to see there are myriads of types of attraction. I'm culpable for the deaths, it was my duty of care, it was my failure, I take full responsibility.

20. STARBUCKS

In a coffee shop, on Oxford Street, in London, in the UK; a young woman, Sheila, perched herself on a tall stool. Her older sister and her sister's best friend, who was visibly pregnant, stayed standing beside her chatting to each other. She didn't mind being excluded from their conversation because she wasn't that interested in the logistics of a future baby shower. Beside Sheila, to her left-hand side, was a shelf holding her chocolate milkshake, with a straw, in its see-through and green single-use plastic take-away container – even though she was 'drinking in'.

On the other side, a long queue of people had built up because the blond barista, who had served her earlier, was now clearing and wiping tables for new customers. He placed the used paper and plastic cups on a black tray and dumped them into a non-recycling bin. He looked dishy in his dark clothes under a green apron.

A man, with a Met identification card dangling around his neck, moved forward to stand beside Shelia. He looked tired. His wait was long; there were six people ahead of him and the queue was not moving. He mumbled something about 'brunch' and 'I could boil an egg ... no ... bake a loaf in the time this is taking.'

Shelia had been taught as a child not to talk to strangers, particularly if they were distressed or angry. She examined him properly. He was quite a bit older than the sexy barista; his dark hair thinning; the worn jacket of his uniform rode up slightly at his back creating an arc of material that looked like it poured into his pockets; his tie was pulled down to reveal two undone top buttons; a pen was placed behind his ear.

He raised his eyebrows on seeing her watch him. 'God, if this takes any longer it'll end up being another night of no sleep.'

'I heard crime doesn't sleep,' Sheila giggled, indicating towards his Met police emblem.

'Tell me about it!' He blew out his breath.

Maybe she shouldn't have said anything and got into a conversation but he looked normal enough. Sheila continued: 'You must have seen a few things in your time?'

'Yeah ... Well, my favourite case was Jenson Ellam, you probably heard of him?'

She shook her head, no, then picked up her milkshake. She put the straw into her mouth but took it out again as the policeman spoke.

'I was promoted after ... and offered counselling.'

She was curious. 'Who was he?'

'I can tell you as it was highly reported. Before he made it big, Jenson Ellam used to do a lot of his early work from a Starbucks, funnily enough. He made his money in antivirus software. Some say he made the malware too ... Well, with so much money, power and technology at his disposal it was no wonder Ellam thought of himself as a god ... He bought up hardware firms, science labs, import/export businesses and then got into the illicit trade of human trafficking, women. He paid good money up front, they were all willing participants, *at first.*' The policeman looked intently at Sheila; he must have seen interest: 'Ellam said he would take good care of the fit young women. Help them get pregnant ...'

Sheila was surprised by the turn of the man's story. She hadn't heard about this at all. 'What do you mean?'

The policeman looked around. His voice quietened so only she could hear. 'Unbeknownst to the women, he took them into his *care* alright!'

Sheila was sceptical. She wondered if he was pulling her leg as she supped chocolate milk up through her straw. It tasted a bit odd.

'First, one of his medico-science companies advertised an "experimental fertility treatment" with "a selection of elite pre-investigated donors" – he was the *expert* who told his victims they would have a better than free treatment – they would be paid handsomely. Then when the —'

'There's no such thing as a free lunch.' She put her milkshake back on the shelf.

'Indeed ...'

'Sorry, I interrupted you.'

'No free lunch, or any lunch at all here, at this rate! ... You are right, that's what caught my attention too. You're clever.'

'I guess you're now going to tell me he didn't use "a selection of",' her hands rose as she mimed quotation marks accompanied by a smile, 'elite male donors he promised, did he?'

'That's right too. Clever girl.' The policeman moved an inch closer to her. 'And Ellam, wasn't stupid, he knew once the babies were born their DNA could lead to his undoing.'

'So, therefore …'

'After eight months these women disappeared into a life they could never have imagined … Before we caught him, he'd kidnapped hundreds of them.'

'Hundreds, that's … too weird!' Shelia was finding the conversation creepy. She wanted to know more but felt the policemen might be just trying to impress her, creep her out or both. She considered saying she wanted to be with her friends and turning her back on him. Her sister and her sister's friend were still discussing babies. It'll be fine, he's a policeman after all. Isn't he?

'Yup. He had it all planned out. But also so much more … he froze them. It's called cryogenics.'

Sheila thought the man must be making this up. 'Cryogenics?' If she stood up that would initiate her sister and sister's friend to return to shopping. But, if they tried to walk out of the coffee shop now, he would be in their direct way.

'Yup. Then, well, it doesn't bear thinking about …'

'Is that even possible? Isn't cryogenics the stuff of science fiction?'

'Apparently not.' The man pulled a folded-up piece of paper

from his pocket and opened it up to show her a highly smudged photocopy of a *Nature* article: No Age Old White Hairs on Reawakening From Ten Thousand Days and Nights of Cryogenics. 'Science fact now.' And, as if that proved everything, he put his article away.

Sheila picked up her milkshake again. She took a sip but it still tasted odd. Maybe the milk the barista had used had been going off? She should complain? Not the best introduction to the blond guy.

The policeman continued, 'Ellam thought the planet was doomed so he had 150 space vehicles built. And each time he had collected four 'eight-month' mothers-to-be (three girl and one boy foetuses) a space vehicle would be blast off.'

'But surely —' she said.

'The mission was not something like going up and then back down again. Oh no! Simply orbiting the earth, or flying people to the moon, wasn't Jenson Ellam's style. He thought of these crafts as seedpods to carry his children on a long, long journey.'

'Those poor women ...'

'Their destination was one of the planets that his people had identified, in a distant galaxy, suitable to human colonisation. God help them!'

'Shit!' Sheila shivered. How could anyone treat women in that way?

'Shit indeed.'

The queue shuffled forward.

The policeman whispered, but his words were still audible to

Sheila: 'They're still out there – on those spaceships – travelling towards some godforsaken place.'

'Can't we get them back with our technology?'

'Oh no …We can't get them back. These women will wake up God knows where! And, God knows when! What they feel or do is anyone's guess!' He made hand movements in time with his words to emphasise the end of each sentence.

'Isn't there any way of turning around or even contacting the spaceships?'

'Ellam wasn't stupid. All the spacecraft are on auto-pilot. As the women are frozen until arrival, nobody human to talk to. The onboard computers ignore all our messages.'

Sheila tried to imagine herself waking on a rocket ship on some far distant planet, she couldn't. She felt anger rising: 'There was no consent for any of that!'

'Indeed! All is lost of their previous lives, Jenson stole that. They were seduced by the money he paid them, not that the mothers will have any ability to spend any of it. They have left this dying planet well behind.'

'More like kidnapped to me.'

'Yes, you are right. And, he's where he should be, locked up. It was the complaints of several of the parents of the mothers-to-be that tipped us off. The last handful of women are the lucky ones. We rescued them before they got shot up into space.'

Sheila shifted in her seat. 'What happened to them and their babies?'

'Too late for any emergency abortions. They have his children to look after now. They'll receive generous compensation for being impregnated. He'll be paying for those kids born on Earth up until his end, not that money was ever an issue for him.'

'What about Jenson?'

'I built the case against him, bringing in specialist scientific help. When we had enough for a warrant to board a spacecraft, we found four frozen women. The same day we went into his Bishop's Avenue mansion and I cuffed him. I felt great that day. But come the trial, we could only do him on the four counts of kidnap and false imprisonment. We just didn't have the detailed evidence – that's long gone. He's in a secure hospital now. Shame, if he gets out for his later life.'

The queue began to move forward and the policeman with it. Shelia looked out for the attractive blond barista at the counter. Before she spotted him, from behind her, her sister said: 'Five minutes and then we will return to the shops, yeah?'

'Great.' Sheila would have taken her attention back to her sister and her sister's best friend, but they started complaining about one or other of their boyfriends.

The policeman had reached the front of the queue and Shelia was pleased to see he was served by the blond barista. She turned her head to better hear the policeman giving his order. She only heard part of the conversation.

'What's that you say?'

'I'm sorry, sir. We are all out of —'

'None left!'

'No … And none of our egg sandwiches are environmentally friendly, sir.' The barista shrugged his shoulders; his attitude nonchalant as if he knows he doesn't need to prove himself to anyone.

There was disappointment in the policeman's voice and he made a dismissive flick with his hand. 'Well in that case, I'll have a medium black coffee with —'

The barista began to educate him about the names of the different sized cups. 'The venti is a 20fl oz drink, it's our largest size for hot drinks. A grande is close to a medium, is that what you want?'

'I don't want a grande, give me a medium black —'

'The tall is smaller. While a small is an 8fl oz drink.' The barista's voice was a monotone. He had physical attributes to rely on – gaining attention must be easy – not so attractive after all.

'I'll just have a salad,' said the policeman.

21. POP-UP SADNESS

Even though it is ever present, we hide death away in our empty cemeteries. We must look forward not back, strive for a future, create a legacy, make history.

*

Carol rests a bunch of off-white roses on the coffee shop's outside table to strip off the labels from the cellophane wrapping. The instructions on how to keep the roses healthy and price tag with barcode are dropped to the ground, adding to the litter in the street. I don't comment. Around the corner, a burnt-out car sits in front of sheltered housing.

Carol had told me how strongly she felt she needed to do something. I wanted to say: I don't want to intrude. She said, 'I can't go on my own.' I put a hand to her shoulder, 'Of course, I'll accompany you.'

Two nights previously the car crashed here killing all three of the young people inside. Metal fencing had been erected around the scene. People have been drawn to this spot bringing flowers to turn it into a makeshift shrine.

The display now contains multiple bunches and raw messages. Carol can't ignore it; she wants to be connected to the death too. As we approach, four people are already there, milling about looking at the flowers and reading the messages. She sticks her roses, with other bouquets and a few single blossoms, into the fence.

I take a cursory look at painful words written about a 'brother lost', children who 'no longer have a father' and 'friendship broken'; confusion expressed in 'angels' and 'meeting up with Raoul, Stef and Eric again.'

Carol can't stop herself saying out aloud: 'It could happen to anyone.'

A fellow mourner, a man, replies: 'It is so out of the ordinary ... For Raoul, death wasn't final so the struggle didn`t matter. He will be reincarnated.'

'You knew him?'

'I loved him ... For me, this has left me sad as Raoul never really tried to fulfil his dreams.'

'I'm so sorry,' said Carol.

'Yes, that's why I'm angry ... He died, as he lived, in narcissistic glory. A candle to a world full of moths, people like me.'

At the foot of the shrine, Carol points to open beer cans; cigarette stubs with ash; and, unlit and half used candles. The objects look positioned in an organised way, as if a tribute. The open beer cans and smoked cigarettes aren't out of place; presumably left as a tribute; representing something about the three dead who had been driving home from a nightclub.

*

Three months later, Carol and I return to the site. The metal fencing still surrounds the damaged building but the long dead flowers and other detritus has been removed.

The mourning has gone elsewhere.

*

Why have I written this piece? Like Carol, like the quarter of a million people who queued to see the queen lying in state, I couldn't ignore a pop-up shrine. Like them, I didn't know the dead person. Like Carol, for some reason, I too want to acknowledge death.

22. WE ARE SO MUCH MORE CIVILIZED

Tom had packed all the necessary paperwork into a see-through folder and carried it under his arm as he made his way to the first-floor lobby. He knew he looked smart in his grey suit and blue tie.

As he waited for the lift, he checked his watch. *I should be about on time.* His hands felt tingly as his anxiety grew. At today's senior managers' meeting he was to be the second person to present – the third item on the agenda. Arriving late would not be a good look; he didn't want anything to get in the way of him getting the promotion he deserved.

The lift, going up, arrived. The doors opened to reveal a single occupant, a tall man in fawn and black clothes.

Tom got in and pressed the 'four' button. The meeting was on the fourth floor as the fifth, including the board room, was being redecorated. The lift went up to the second floor. The doors opened but nobody got in or out. The doors closed.

The lift rose towards the third. The light flickered then the lift jolted to a halt. The light went out completely and then came back on again. *Today! This happens today!*

Tom pressed the 'four' button a couple of times. Nothing happened. 'Bloody lift!' Tom checked his watch again.

'It could be a long day,' the tall man said as he edged ever so slightly towards the rear of the lift.

'I really hope not. I've a meeting which started about …' Tom looked at his watch again '… a minute ago.'

'Stay calm … We've lost power, probably a power cut. We'll be stuck here between two and three for a little while.'

'No, no, this can't be happening to me!' Tom leant over and pushed the emergency alarm.

'That's not going to help.'

'We need to do something. The emergency button is there for a reason. We need to raise the alarm.'

'Do you see any light around the buttons?'

'No. Why the —'

'We are working on the back-up power now. It'll all get sorted out soon enough. That'll be their priority … You in some sort of rush?'

'I've a meeting on fourth. God, I'm going to get roasted by the Founder.' *Why do I fret so much about my career?*

'He's not that bad.'

Tom took a closer look at the bulky man: His face was chiselled. He wore a light wool overcoat with a belt at the waist, the buttons were hidden. 'You a friend of Mr Haig?'

'I wouldn't say friend,' said the man.

'Oh. I am ... My name is Tom by the way ... I work in sales ... Top salesman in March.' Tom knew he was chattering out of nerves; he didn't want to think about how his late arrival would look.

'Good for you.'

'I'm sorry?'

The man grinned: 'Good for you, working the Mortimer account.'

What? How does he know my business?

The man pointed at my see-through folder.

My surprise must have shown. 'Err ... What floor do you want?'

'One before you. Third.'

He seems to enjoy my discomfort. 'Oh, you must know Jenny Nicolson? She should be at my meeting.'

'We've never had a long conversation.'

Tom stretched his arms, moved his see-through folder from left to right under arm, before looking at his watch again. *I'm going to be really late.* He wondered whether he should call the boss's PA to say he was stuck. In reflex to the sweat at his collar, he reached up to wipe around his neck. 'It's hot in here.'

'Not as hot as the desert ...'

The man wore heavy-duty leather combat boots under his fawn trousers. *Oh my God it's him! I'm trapped in a lift with him! The Founder's special aide, who'd been sent in to the Aberdeen office after the accusations surfaced. It was never made clear how he cleaned that up. It all was very quiet after.* Tom decided not to let on he had heard about the man. Perhaps he could draw him out. 'So, what do you actually do apart from being Mr. Haig's "wouldn't say friend"?'

'I'm a problem solver, a troubleshooter, so to speak.'

'So to speak?'

'I get paid to deal with … in polite circles, it's called waste management.'

'And what is that in impolite circles?'

'Oh … mercenary.'

'What? Really? Do we still need mercenaries nowadays?'

'Oh yes. Here, we are oh so much more civilized, but … that's what history brings to a country.'

'Are … are we?'

'Of course, when I fought in Afghanistan, there was just five of us against a hundred savages.'

That sounds like the plot of Zulu. 'No … Did you actually kill anyone?'

'I don't like to talk about it in that way. It's a job. But, yes, I've killed dozens of men and maimed a score more.'

I don't believe a word of this. The man talks of adventures as if they are fact. More like tall tales or simply lies.

Tom scratched the bridge of his nose. 'And that makes us more civilized?'

'Oh no … All is peaceful here, but you can never be sure what is in the offing … You must always keep vigilant.'

Tom looked at the man squarely in the face. 'Steve Haig says you have never left Britain.'

The man wore a poker face. 'So, you have heard about me …

Well, Steve doesn't know everything.'

I can smell something? 'Steve says you would be too scared to go and fight.' *Is that musk?*

'Let me tell you; it does scare me … but it also excites me. And I find all this,' the man indicated around him with his hands, 'the unreal world.'

Conflict between males can generate musk. The man's presence dominated the small space. *Shit! What if I've got this all wrong? What if he really is a killer!*

The man asked, 'And what else does Steve say?'

Shit! Tom was on edge, he stammered: 'He says you ha … have an ea … eagle tattoo.'

'Yes, I have a large eagle on my back. They are solitary, masters of their own destiny.'

'Is … is … t … t … that you?' Tom knew his nerves were causing him to stutter.

'They are the hunter, swooping down and ripping into prey with beak and claw. The top of the food chain. I can relate to that.'

Tom swallowed hard. 'Ha … have you really killed anyone?'

The man lifted his right fist. He had big hands. 'I've crushed a man with just this one hand.' He paused.

Tom felt a wave of claustrophobia. The musk oppressive and overpowering. *I'm in a compromised space. Was this man waiting for me to board this lift? Have I done something wrong? Could Steve want to do me in as I know too much? There is plastic sheeting everywhere on the fifth floor.*

The man smiled at Tom. 'Steve insists I do not kill anyone

here at headquarters.'

The light flickered and the lift started up; the power had only been off for four to five minutes. The tall man edged ever so slightly towards the front of the lift, beside Tom.

The lift ascended to the third floor, where the doors opened and Jenny Nicolson was waiting holding a pile of green Manilla files. She looked like she had been fretting; a little of her usually immaculate hair was out of place. *It's a relief to see a familiar face.*

The man stepped out. 'Nice meeting you … T … T … Tom. Say hi to Steve.'

Jenny got in. 'At least I'm not going to be the only one late.'

'Yeah … the meeting.' Tom pressed the 'four' button one more time.

23. MEN ARE SO DIFFERENT, AREN`T THEY?

It was a spring day within winter. The sun shone brightly but the few city plants hadn`t begun to blossom.

Two women sat chatting behind the plate glass window of 'Chez Brasserie – London'. Both were drinking gin and tonics, each accompanied by ice and a slice. 'Talk of the Town' by The Pretenders was playing quietly in the background. It was the end of February 1993.

Flushed red in her cheeks Joyce leaned towards her and exclaimed: 'Men are so different, aren`t they, Mary? ... From us, I mean ... Well ... I thought he was joking at first. I could choke couldn`t I? I mean how could he ask me to do something like that?' This was the third time Mary had heard Joyce's anecdote, she knew she wasn't expecting a response. Mary looked out the spotlessly clean window.

I could count the cracks in that pavement ... A young woman passed outside. She was lightly bouncing in her DMs and smiling. Her arced mouth showed off a top row of teeth and pushed up her cheeks, forming a crease under her eyes and a spray of little lines at their sides. She was happy in the unexpected sunshine. A green woolly scarf was worn around her neck and a matching knitted jumper stuck out from under her off-grey leather jacket. She tapped the bollards at the edge of the pavement with her newspaper as she went by.

Joyce brought Mary back to the restaurant: 'It's not as if we are dreamy-eyed teenagers anymore!' Joyce is the big talker.

Clicking her fingers, Mary called out: 'Garçon.' She caught the attention of the black and white uniformed waiter. He took his order book out from his apron's pocket: 'You are ready to order, oui?'

'We'll start by sharing the asparagus spears, then I'll have the partridge and you're having the salmon with the hot dill hollandaise, aren't you Joyce?'

'Yes … and a mixed salad … and a single portion of new potatoes to share.'

Mary assumed Joyce ordered the salad to give a balance of roughage against the starchy carbohydrates of her potatoes, and the protein and fat in the salmon and sauce.

Both women closed their menus and handed them to the waiter. 'Oh, can we have the salad's dressing on the side? A bottle of the white Rioja. And some tap water,' said Mary.

'Oui madam.' The waiter bowed his head, before walking away.

'John always says he was attracted to me from the first

moment he set eyes on me. He stared at me, the girl in the corner seat of a railway carriage,' Joyce told Mary. 'It was my hands, he said. I wore two rings on either hand at the time. Whether they were of a Celtic or a gothic style, I chose the rings because of their intricate and delicate silverwork. He was attracted to my hands. Apparently, I was twisting my hair around my fingers and looking at it. I threaded the braid through my fingers again and again. In those days, they were long slender fingers with blazing red fingernails, each careful grown and shaped before being painted. He said I looked like I was deep in thought of another place, another time. And he said he wished he could have been there with me. He can be sweet when he wants to be!'

Mary drained the end of her gin and tonic. The lemon slice fell from the top to the bottom in the glass, as she put it down on the table.

Joyce leant in. 'Apparently, I pulled my fingers down the strand, brushed my mouth with its ends and put my hair into my mouth. Then his eyes met mine. He says my hands let go of my hair and I held them in front of me crossed within my lap. I don`t believe I put it in my mouth but he talked to me anyway, and that was over twenty-five year ago. Doesn`t time fly?'

'So impractical, long nails!' Mary pushed her empty gin and tonic glass to the centre of the table.

'Indeed, and artificial looking! That`s why I`m au naturel now.' Joyce put her hands down on the table top as if to prove what she had said: 'I mean it never really was me anyway.' Joyce carried on with her anecdote.

Why is she telling me all this again? Is she boasting? Mary listened while looking out the window.

A dark-haired woman wearing patent-leather ankle boots with buckles and a long girlie pink coat went towards the bread shop across the road. From under her coat could be seen a little of a loose leopard-print scarf and the darkest of Windsor-blue cuffs and trousers. She entered the shop. In the window, the breads were piled high: Whites, light browns and yellows. Challahs and soft rolls. Large and small bloomers. Seedy Greek, French crusty and French sticks. The woman came out of the shop holding an uncut white loaf in a paper bag. In the street, as she walked away, she held the loaf up to her nose and smelt it.

Mary turned away from the window scene. She observed the expensive print dress Joyce was wearing had a design that looked like paint splashes of the boldest colours.

Joyce twiddled with her wedding ring. 'You know at first I'd liked it when he was a bit masterful. It would seem all wrong now though. I know I'm really lucky, he's such a nice man. He is kind, and considerate, and caring with the children. You know what he said to me the other day? That he feels like the china ornaments we have on our mantelpiece. He's funny.'

There was movement at their table as the waiter arrived with Rioja, two long-stemmed wine glasses and an ice bucket on a stand. 'Would you like to taste the wine, madame?'

Joyce indicated towards Mary then picked up her gin and

tonic and took a sip.

The waiter pulled a corkscrew from his pocket. He cut the foil from the top of the bottle then screwed and pulled out the cork. He put a tea towel around the bottom of bottle and showed off the label to Mary.

'Yup!'

He poured a tiny amount of the pale-yellow liquid into Mary's tall stemmed glass. She picked it up, smelt a hint of melon, then drunk it down.

'Lovely.' She nodded.

The waiter went to pour Joyce's glass.

'I'll have mine with the main,' said Joyce.

The waiter went back to Mary's glass and poured her a half glass, put the open bottle in the ice bucket and retreated. He left the gin and tonic glasses on the table. Shortly after he returned with bread and butter and the asparagus first course.

'Did you hear Di wants a divorce?' said Mary.

'I don't blame her.'

They ate for two minutes in silence. Joyce talked more about John. Mary stopped herself from tutting. Instead, she listened, ate and watched what was going on outside.

A business woman, with a shapely body and legs, stopped directly outside the window asking for directions from a policeman. He looked very young, standing upright, in his uniform. He had three stripes on his sleeve so he must have been a sergeant. Her long frizzy red hair was held in place by a black clasp;

it matched her crimson suit. She also wore a white blouse, black seamed stockings, heavy gold jewellery and red high-heeled shoes. She carried an A-Z and a shiny black attaché case in her right hand. As she talked, she gently scratched her cheek with the second finger of her left hand, then she used it to twice brush down the length of her nose, a nose that was long and fine with a slightly bigger than expected end. The finger then went back up and around her eye smoothing her dark brow.

The first course plates and cutlery were cleared away. Mary asked Joyce: 'Did you see that nature programme last night on the wild cats of Scotland? Beautiful.'

Joyce shook her head in the negative and poured what was left in her gin and tonic glass into her mouth.

'Isn't that just lemon-tasting water?'

'Yes.' Joyce smiled. 'Time for some wine for me.'

As Joyce leant towards the ice bucket the waiter appeared. He filled both the women's wine glasses, put the bottle back in the ice bucket and backed away, removing the two empty aperitif glasses from the table.

Mary tried a different question: 'How are the children?'

'Oh fine. A handful as usual. We have a nanny now.'

'Really?'

'John told me business is booming and I thought why not! Not that Jane needs it … she's thirteen, wants to take up horse riding'

'That's going to cost you isn't it?'

'Yes, *and* as soon as we've bought all the gear, she'll be bored of it and want to do something else. We should never have given her a My Little Pony when she was little. And then there are the music lessons! Jane and Peter are learning the piano while Janet – she has to be different – she says she wants to learn the clarinet.'

There was a flurry of activity at their table, carried out by two men in the black and white uniforms.

Outside a male cyclist in a black face mask, blue cagoule, and lime accessories (helmet and rucksack) whizzed by.

Men's clothes are so different.

As the food arrived, Mary smelt the sweet pear liquor sauce that the partridge came in. On the other white plate, the salmon's flesh had been poached pink. The side of new potatoes arrived in a white china bowl, still steaming from the kitchen; a knob of melting butter and cut parsley put a yellow sheen with green flakes on to their skins. The mixed salad, in a matching white bowl, was lettuce, tomatoes, shallots and black olives. A tiny white jug full of French dressing was placed beside the salad.

The original waiter asked to serve some more wine. Both women gave assent by nodding. The waiter half-filled both the women's glasses. The sound it made was a soft glug-glug-glugging, stop and again glug-glug-glug. He placed the bottle back in the ice bucket, standing beside their table.

As she drank, Mary noticed the lipstick grease she left on the lip of her glass.

Into the new calm, of course Joyce was the first to speak. 'John and I have given up eating red meat since all these scares about BSE. It's terrible the way they treat animals nowadays and all the chemicals and hormones used to make them bigger.'

'You're not going to become a vegetarian on me, are you?'

'Oh no, heaven forbid, it's for health reasons.'

Fifteen minutes later, their waiter cleared away dishes and asked if they wanted dessert.

For pudding, Mary had two varieties of ice cream covered in cherry sauce, while Joyce wolfed down a burnt-sienna coloured chocolate gateau covered in whipped cream.

Outside, a white-haired woman, aged somewhere in her mid-sixties aggressively went by. She was walking the dog. Or to be more precise, being led by a black, white and grey mongrel. She wore scarlet lipstick, darkened glasses and a short grey skirt. Due to the cold this showed her long legs mottled with a red pink hue; but still, she displayed the lower half of a thigh and calf – good muscle tone for her age. She wore low light-green suede heels on her feet. She stopped and stroked her dog then looked in at the window, stared at them, before disappearing.

'That skirt was far too short for her,' commented Joyce.

Mary leant down and reached under her chair to her floppy handbag. She had to move her umbrella to get to it. 'I wouldn't show my legs off if I was her. She's still thinks she's young.'

After unzipping the bag, Mary withdrew a packet of cigarettes and a thin, streamlined, gold lighter. The cigarettes were in a red packet with two yellow strips. She took out a 120 mm dark-brown wrapped More.

Mary called over the waiter again: 'Garçon!'

They ordered two cappuccinos.

When Mary pushed the button on the side of the lighter, a clear blue flame emanated from the hole on the top. She offered Joyce a cigarette, which was at first declined but then taken up. Cupping her hand around her friend's cigarette she lit it, and with the same action she lit her own.

Joyce leant forward putting both her elbows on to the table. With lips pursed, she drew in smoke; sucking deeply, holding, and then letting it out with a sigh.

Mary sat back on her chair and took shallow breaths. Feeling relaxed, she allowed her right shoe to come off the back of her foot; she scratched her right heel with the point of her left shoe.

The cappuccinos arrived. Joyce mixed up the frothy cream, chocolate and coffee and downed it hot. Mary played with her drink; she first ate the cream topping, digging her way to the coffee and then supped a spoonful at a time.

Frankie Goes To Hollywood's 'The Power of Love' started up, playing out of a nearby speaker, the sound was louder than before.

Joyce tutted.

'The music shouldn't be so loud in these places,' said Mary.

In the window, Mary caught a reflection from inside the

restaurant. A woman wearing a long silk amethyst dress walked behind them, sparkling light danced off her dangly earrings as the beautiful smell of jasmine perfume wafted through the air.

It's time to go home. Mary reached under her chair to pick up her bag and brolly. 'I've so much to do later.' She put a hand in the air and mimed to the waiter the signing of a cheque. Smiling at Joyce she joked: 'I've had too much excitement for one afternoon.'

The waiter came over with the bill, inside a small green lacquered box; 'Madam.'

He's been polite and attentive. A waiter is so different from a waitress. We'll leave a nice tip.

24. CHÂTEAU DE MARVILLE

Madame Elante Pompidou attended worship at the cathedral every evening. It was the right thing to do.

The Thursday before Christmas, she threw on a bonnet, long coat and galoshes to protect herself from the weather. Claude, her husband, was tending the garden. Elante told him: 'Go indoors and get dry, this instant!' Claude complied.

As she walked the short distance toward the red sandstone of the cathedral, the wind was blowing so strongly Elante had to hold a hand on top of her bonnet. Rain began to pitter-patter around her, and a dog tied up outside the cathedral howled. The rain looked like it was about to turn heavy; Elante was pleased to enter the Holy place through solid black doors.

Inside, looking down, there were both stern agents of God's vengeance and stone angels offering hope. To Elante, there was almost a Byzantine feel. How can anyone be an atheist when confronted with such beauty – it's jaw dropping.

The other worshippers were also wrapped in warm clothing,

scarves and winter boots. There was a handsome old man Elante had not seen before, in a woollen coat, thick socks and gloves.

Candles displayed an eerie light. She looked up to Heaven, marble columns held up an unadorned red sandstone high ceiling, giving a feeling of majestic space. It's awe inspiring. Elante shivered, imagining the sandstone soaking up all the water from the storm outside.

The service was music, preaching and liturgy. The evensong so beautiful when it came.

Elante knelt on a colourful fleur-de-lys embroidered cushion to whisper her prayers: 'Jesus died on the cross for my sins. I pray I am a good Christian, Lord. Thank you for the food you put on my family's table. But I am struggling. How can I practise humility and gratitude when I am a slave to sin? I lust after sensual delight daily.' She looked towards the stranger before continuing quietly: 'I pray and pray but still think evil thoughts at times. I can even have doubts about my beliefs, questioning your very existence. I feel guilty now vocalising that.'

Between her whispered words she heard from God: 'Watch out for Claude.'

*

Returning to the château at 9 o'clock, Elante headed straight to the kitchen. Something about the half-light felt strangely unfamiliar to her. Her tabby cat lay in the dog's basket, looking pleased with herself. The net curtain was twitching. Elante removed her bonnet and shook damp from it. She hung her coat off the back of a chair. She swapped her galoshes for slippers.

Outside the window stained in dirt, swaying branches groped about. When a thin branch reached out to scratch against the glass, Elante's hands began to shake. 'Is that you God? What do you want from me? … I am your servant.'

She knelt to pray but instead of talking to God, she saw a black apparition. She didn't believe what she saw was possible – there was a deep blackness that grew within the shadow. She looked twice but it persisted. Her eyes then got stuck staring at the dark poisoning all in its wake. It preyed on her soul.

A distraction was needed. She used all of her courage to make a cup of tea. She pulled out the drawer for a teaspoon and saw the knife. Looking up, in the reflection in the window, lines crisscrossed her drawn face. Drinking her tea steadied her nerves.

Elante went up the hallway stairs; her tabby cat followed; no sound came from any of the padded feet. The stairs, with black and white carpet and wooden banister, went up to a gallery area, where Elante's grandfather (her father's father) had started the display of family photos. She ignored her forebears and she ignored the newer photos of her and Claude – their wedding day, them relaxed on holiday and a single portrait photo of each of them.

She entered the bedroom she had shared with her husband for the last twenty-two years. The cat curled up in a warmest corner by the radiator. Elante disrobed and carefully piled up her clothes on the green velvet chair on her side of the bed. There was a gleam among her clothes.

She moved on to the bathroom to brush her teeth and hair. There were sounds of movement from the bed that told her she had disturbed her husband.

From the four-poster, she heard a sleepy voice tell her: 'Hurry up, dear. Come to bed.' He only lay his head back on his pillow when she turned off the light.

Elante climbed into bed beside him. 'Claude, Claude, are you awake?'

'Yes?' He questioned.

'Well,' she murmured, 'in church tonight God spoke to warn me.'

Claude didn't answer.

She said: 'I have an early Christ Mass present for you Claude.'

25. TIT FOR TAT

First, yellow and gold thread antennae appeared, followed quickly by a black head with two white dot eyes.

'Don't be scared,' said Daddy. 'Look at the dark-green-and-wood-coloured wings.'

I had been running around the kitchen. All I could see in Daddy's big hand were the eyes looking back at me; then I took in the wings with bright green spots and I noticed a black painted strip down the bug's back which cut straight through the wings.

I reached out to touch it.

'Oh, be careful!' he said.

I pulled my hand back.

'Hold your hand flat. Don't clench it in your fist.' Daddy's belly pushed out at an open button of his shirt, with a few black hairs sticking out just the same as the antennae.

He gently gave the bug to me. It was light and filled half my palm. The surface texture was smooth and consistent. It felt like it would jump out if I poked it with a finger.

'Why have you bought a green bug, Daddy?'

'Look, it's fun.' He took it back from me and stuck it to the fridge. 'A dragon fly!'

'What's the point of that, Daddy?'

'It's a fridge magnet.'

'So?' I have asked him all sorts of questions before: where do the clouds come from; why does it get dark at night time; how far is it to the moon; does anyone live there? Most of the time, Daddy had some sort of answer. Daddy is the cleverest man in the whole world!

But this time, he didn't answer my 'So?' He took the dragon fly off the fridge and flipped it on to its back. 'Now look it can't move.'

I pointed at the tiny words on the underside. 'What does it say Daddy?'

'It says it was made in China ... I thought it would cheer up the kitchen.'

'Does Mummy like it?'

'Look, if she can have a sign saying "STEP AWAY FROM THE FRIDGE, LARDASS!" I can have this little chappy.'

'What sort of dragon fly is it, Daddy?'

'You have so many questions ... Come on, now, it's time for you to get ready for bed.'

'No!'

'Yes, we've had our supper and a night time walk, haven't we?'

'Yes.'

'So … time to go upstairs, brush your teeth and put on your PJs. If you are in your bed in ten minutes I'll tell you a story. Tit for tat …'

*

Waiting in bed, I felt tired.

Eventually Daddy came into my bedroom. He ignored the armchair and sat down on the side of my bed, his belly pushed up against me like a cushion.

My eyelids drooped, but I was still able to ask: 'Daddy. Do you believe in dragons?'

'Hmmmmmm. Dragon-flies?'

'Don't be silly Daddy. Dragon dragons!'

Funny you should ask. Now I'm gonna tell you something amazing. Something you will find unbelievable. Listen carefully …'

Daddy paused, he took forever. I knew he wanted me to go to sleep but I didn't want to sleep, I wanted a story. I broke the silence: 'Daddy, I'm listening carefully. Very carefully.' I rubbed at my face with my hand to push the sleep away.

'Yes, yes,' he replied. 'I am just gathering my thoughts. Let's see. Yes. The big green scaly monster came towards me ... I had a shotgun in my hands.'

'Did you, Daddy?' I have heard so many of his adventures of derring-do. He is heroic. But facing down a dragon was something else!

'Shh! Dragons are part of the reptile family ... Until up close, I was —'

192

'Did you kill him?'

'It was a her and she got up on powerful hind legs. I felt she wanted to hug and slobber all over me. I could see her teeth and the dribble. I was fearful being so close to this dragon.'

'What did you do Daddy?' I yawned.

'It's your sleep time.'

'No.'

'You are so curious. The prerogative of ... When I was young, I was always looking for a manual for life in the books I read. You should try reading in bed.'

'What did you do with the dragon, Daddy?'

He rummaged in his pockets and pulled out two Chupa Chups. 'Would you like one of these?'

'Yeah.'

'Don't tell your mother. She'll kill me. You've already brushed your teeth.'

'Chupa Chup, please!' I held out my hand.

'I'll only give it to you if you promise to go to sleep and ask no more questions.'

'Oh-no, tell me the end of the story.'

Daddy held the Chupa Chups away from me before continuing, 'I won't pretend I wasn't frightened. The situation was scary. I freely confess, I thought it is her or me. I pulled back the two triggers.'

'Yes, Daddy?'

'She came forward.'

'Yes?'

'Yes, so close, dribble poured all over my head. But I stood my ground.'

'Did you shoot her?'

'It went through my head. But what if I had shot? She would be lying with legs splayed out on a rocky floor, half a side of her open, red seeping from the wound. She would be dead.'

'So, what did you do? Did you let her live?'

'Yes, son, I married her.'

'Egh?'

Daddy grinned.

'Daddy be serious!' I have overheard Mummy saying more than once: you think you're the funniest man in the World!

'Yes, of course dear … It is just not right to go around killing God's creatures willy-nilly!'

'Can I have one of the Chupa Chups, now?'

Daddy handed me a lollipop.

I ripped off the plastic wrapping.

Daddy switched the light off. 'Goodnight.'

As soon as I put the Chupa Chup in my mouth, I could taste something was wrong. I called out, 'Daddy, this is the sugar free version!'

On his way out of my bedroom, he left the door slightly ajar. 'And you are a clever one because you're a very curious child.'

26. TALL BOY

'Tony's died,' I said in a matter-of-fact voice. I'd found out through an email. I only then realised that I was crying at my desk.

'Oh, that's terrible!' Michelle lay on the sofa reading the Saturday *Guardian* magazine. 'How did he die?'

'There isn't any detail – it just says he "passed away".' I couldn't still the waterworks. 'Why is it that my tears relieve me?'

'We are all physical, Jolian,' said Michelle. 'Tears are useful – they comfort the body.'

*

On the day of the funeral, I was still undecided on whether to go or not. I'd only kept in contact with Tony because he had been a friend of mine at school over four decades earlier. We hadn't socialised since.

I dressed for work.

Michelle's mobile rang. It was her brother Creed. He only rings when he wants something from her. After signing off, she told me: 'I'll be out this afternoon helping Creed.' Again! She still feels responsible for him. Older sisters.

'If Creed had a job, he might have more purpose in life.'

'He's had a hard time —'

'Being ill and disadvantaged —'

'Don't!' She was upset; she caught her long black hair behind her neck and put it into a purple hair tie. She can be stubborn as well as delicate and feminine. Maybe I should have apologised, this disagreement was my fault.

That's when I decided I would attend the funeral after all.

I pulled out the top drawer of my mahogany tallboy. I took out a clean handkerchief and put it into my pocket. I might need it at Tony's.

*

That morning, I worked in the British Library. I ate a sandwich en route to the crematorium. I arrived at the chapel, ten minutes early, at 2.50pm.

The vicar was long-winded in his address. But the heartfelt personal reflections from Tony's son were powerful.

I went on to the reception as I knew Michelle was going to be out in the afternoon. It was held in a large upstairs room at the William IV, up steps covered in a sticky green carpet.

We hung our coats on a rollable coat rail, at the top of the stairs, then Tony's wife and their son, their only child, greeted mourners in a small line, along with the vicar. Colly was there at the front, the first to talk to Tony's wife. I hadn't seen him for over a decade. I hoped to avoid him, but knew it would be difficult.

I said to the vicar, 'Lovely service.' I didn't mean his bit.

The vicar said something like, 'God can bring solace at a difficult time.'

I grunted before being moved on to Tony's son.

'Your personal reflections of your dad were very moving.'

'Thanks,' said Tony's son.

I wanted to offer some comfort: 'I think there is a real need to look after yourself in difficult times like this.' Out loud, my message of comfort sounded like a platitude.

'Yeah, I guess,' he replied looking to the person behind me.

The line moved forward. I was next standing in front of Tony's wife. Neither of us seemed to want to speak first so I said: 'Condolences. We were very sorry to hear about Tony ...' Conversation was stilted. I don't think she knew who I was. I said: 'Michelle sends her love.'

'Thank you for coming,' she said.

A waitress handed me a glass of white wine and I knew I was meant to start to circulate. Unfortunately, Colly stood right in front of me. He showed off his success in his clothes – a white creaseless cravat (who wears a cravat!), a red-with-gold braid shirt, a gleaming black leather long coat and a floppy hat failing to hide grey hair – but he was the same boy I knew back at school.

He squinted, through expensive specs, to examine me with his beady green shortsighted eyes. His specs were held by ears bigger than I remember. There were new lines and bags in his face.

'Shorty!' he smiled with narrow lips: 'How are you, old boy?

You have put on some weight I see. Ha! Ha!'

I didn't laugh along. 'It's still Jolian.'

'Yes, yes, of course.' He stepped forward, wine glass in hand. He was far too close for comfort; I could feel the air coming to and from his prominent nostrils. Any closer and I'd be touched up by the stubble on his red, ruddy face.

'It's good to see you, even in the circumstances.' I started to fidget so I held my right wrist with my other hand. That gave more stability to the hand holding my wine glass.

'Yes, yes.'

'I have —'

'Who is your tailor these days? Those are quite horrible brown corduroys. And that waistcoat!'

'I came straight from the British Library.'

'Don't tell me you have to work in a library. Get out more! Come see one of my plays. *Playboy Hustle* is nominated for an Olivier award.'

I looked around for an escape. 'I have seen —'

'Let me tell you about life as a playwright.'

I tried again. 'I have seen —'

'You are too pale … Have you given up red meat like Tony did?' One of Colly's hands gestured towards a food table; all the nibbles were vegetarian; cucumber sandwiches, quiche, crisps, vegan sausage rolls and pastries.

'No, I —'

'And really! Can't you afford a haircut anymore? My boy, you have to look after yourself or you'll never snatch yourself a yummy wifelet.'

'I have ...' I was about to tell Colly about Michelle but realized the funeral and wake had made me want to be with her all the more, the only important person in my life – she had promised to be home by four. Instead, I pointed to a picture that I had spotted which included young versions of the two of us. The reception was billed as a celebration of Tony's life. There were many photos of him with family and friends, from all the different periods of his life, stuck up on boards. Our photo was within a 'schooldays' section. 'That's us ...'

'Well, I never!' said Colly. 'You looked uncomfortable in your clothes back then too. They just hang on you, don't they?'

I tried to change the subject away from either him putting me down or building himself up: 'Lovely service.'

'Did you hear what the Pope has been saying about my plays?'

The Pope! I couldn't face any more of Colly's nonsense. It had gone four; Michelle should be at home by now. I wanted to go. 'Excuse me, I have to ...'

I turned away from Colly and walked purposefully. When you want to get away you rush. As I grabbed my coat, I barged into a young man in a dark-blue suit. It being Tony's son added to my embarrassment. I apologised profusely and slowly retreated in reverse.

'Don't worry about it,' he said.

The soles of my shoes felt sticky against the carpet. I told myself not to think about what the substances were that made the carpet tacky. I lifted my feet a little higher than normal to ensure my feet touched as little of the surface as possible. Going backwards, I tripped over my own feet.

When you rush you are more likely to have an accident. A silly accident! I lost my balance and felt myself going over and over.

I went down the stairs. It was a nasty fall.

*

Michelle visited me every few days for the first four months.

Over the sound of a machine whirring and hissing, I could hear her and make out shadows moving around in front of me. Michelle told the doctor: 'Spending time with your husband is the minimum a wife can do.'

'You are very good,' he replied. I didn't want to hear him say that. The doctor sounded interested. I know she's more than good.

She gave an embarrassed laugh. I couldn't tell if she liked his comment or not.

My vision was at best a haze. I saw a blurred light strip surrounded by grey – I wonder if it's a light on a ceiling. I must have been on my back looking upwards. I realised the hissing sound, that rhythmic rising and falling in loudness, was from a ventilator. *Is that keeping me alive?*

Michelle told the doctor about a claim she had made against the pub: 'The lawyer said the William IV might be negligent as it had not provided a safe environment.'

I knew she leant over me as I could smell coffee and orange blossom from her favourite perfume, Black Opium. I felt pressure on my arm – I presumed her hand – it gave me a moment of pleasure. The warm feeling was fleeting, she must have removed her hand. I wish I could have seen her lovely face. Michelle is a woman who always looks good; even in a baseball cap! I know I'm lucky to have her.

After Michelle's visit, I heard steps outside, then inside the room. I could not make out the person or people. There was movement close by, something was happening, there was bright light then droplets put into my eyes. Saline? My eyes must have been very dry. Next, the room was cleaned. I didn't want it to be. The smell of Jeyes cleaning fluid, or whatever it was that they used, was a terrible comedown after the Black Opium. I wanted to cry. I wanted that relief. But I couldn't cry. I couldn't even gain that small comfort.

*

I was washed once a day. I'd hear running water then a soapy smell would reach me. Sometimes I have to be cleaned more often, that's usually after the smell of my own urine has reached me first. I feel my sheet and my clothes being removed. My eyes are wiped. Then comes my face and neck, chest and stomach, arms, feet and legs. I hear water being poured away. I'm dried on my front with a towel before a lotion is rubbed on to some parts of my body. I am turned over for the back to be cleaned. It is all so undignified.

Afterwards, if it is the brisk nurse, he will prop me up and ask: 'Would you like to watch some TV?' It's lighthearted, he thinks it's amusing that he is treating me like a normal patient, but I find it annoying. He doesn't wait for a reply, he knows I can't respond. I often hear Neighbours – not a show I'd watch – it must be late afternoon. I feel like I'm being used like a doll and the male nurse has put me in the right position so the TV set has been lined up directly in front of me, but I have no idea. Sometimes I can see shapes but usually it is all a blur, whatever it is in front of me.

*

Another day, over a constant whirr sound and rhythm of beeps, I heard muffled loud laughter; it grates as I'm not part of the joy. There are people moving around me accompanied by fresher air. Nearby, Michelle asked the doctor: 'How has he been?'

'Your husband's condition has stabilised, which is good, but he can't see, hear or feel and he will remain in this state. '

What rubbish! Being paralysed hasn't stopped me hearing you.

'Will he —'

'As he did not recover in the first few months, the prognosis is that no further improvement is expected.'

I felt wretched on hearing I wasn't expected to get better. Then I reconsidered: *He thinks I can't hear – that's a misdiagnosis! My body still feels; the nerve endings in my skin work as does my heart.*

The conversation went to another subject. She told the doctor she had lost her bid for compensation from the William IV. The judge rejected her claim as I had neither been shoved nor barged down the stairs.

*

From that moment on, Michelle visited less – maybe once a week.

It was irritating that because of what the doctor had said to her about my prognosis, Michelle stopped speaking directly to me. I had liked that she spoke to me, read to me, she'd even once sung to me.

*

Michelle and Creed's shapes seemed brightly coloured when they visited together. I wondered if they might be wearing summer clothes.

She joked: 'Jolian's under the beardy Dr Steffen.' I felt a pang of jealousy knowing by the way she said 'beardy' that she liked this man. *Even if gone, I hope I'm not forgotten. I'd like to think I remain, at least, a friend for life?*

'Can I have his tallboy?' asked Creed.

'Yes, of course. He's not going to need it. You can take any clothes that fit you too,' said Michelle.

'I don't think so!' chortled Creed.

It's just objects!

I heard the clatter of a passing trolley competing with the whirring and beeping of the machines. I wanted to hear more of her. Most of all, I wished I could see her. *Michelle, I know you are oh so beautiful! I want to wrap you up in my arms, but I can't. I can't move my hands, legs, eyes or mouth. You are distant, not mine anymore, not to ever be mine again.*

I heard a door and footsteps – someone new had entered the room. 'Is this your brother?' I knew it was Dr Steffen as soon as he spoke. 'Pleased to meet you.'

'Jolian's functions are not coming back, are they?' asked Creed.

'He has more than loss of limb function. He has complete paralysis. No blinking or vertical eye movement.'

'Tell her she needs to get on with her life,' said Creed.

'Jolian has had a traumatic brain injury. If he was in a vegetative state, he could come off life support and be able to breathe on his own and digest food ... But he has lost respiratory control.' *I'm on full life support!*

'You need to get on with your life ... He wouldn't have wanted you in limbo too,' said Creed.

What's he saying?

'We are without specific guidance from Jolian,' said the doctor.

'He wouldn't have wanted to be like this,' said Michelle.

'He never specified "do everything possible" or "do not resuscitate," it'll be up to you,' said the doctor.

'I don't know what to do,' said Michelle.

Don't turn me off!

'Listen to the Doc,' said Creed. 'Jolian's accident was horrific but Sis, it's not you on life support.' The whirring and beeping of the machines had become more pronounced.

'I can't stand him being like this!' said Michelle. 'He can't even shed a tear.

There was a long pause. *Christ! What's going on?*

'Goodbye, Jolian … you were good to me,' said Michelle.

Shit! She's talking directly to me in the past tense. Yes, and you were wonderful too. Weren't we people who were good for each other?

27. CROSSRAIL

My friends call me a history enthusiast but since retirement it is more of a vocation, it gives me purpose. The only way to know one's place in the world is by having an understanding of the past.

I became a member of the Ealing History Society at sixty-five, that was nine years ago. Last December, the chairman resigned through ill health. In January, Captain Timothy Brody, the society's treasurer, and I stood against each other in the election to replace him. I won.

On becoming the chairman, I automatically joined the London Historians. I've particularly enjoyed getting to know fellow enthusiasts at their monthly pub meetings. Friday night in the White Hart was one such occasion.

I dusted down my old office suit and put on a smart shirt and florid tie to go with it. I knew my purpose for the meeting: to drum up opposition to the building of a twenty-storey tower block beside the Hoover Building. The Ealing History Society had already submitted our opposition. I wanted other groups to do likewise. I love Art Deco buildings – I associate them with the jazz age and good times.

At the very start, we had congregated in the Function Room, the chairwoman pointed out: 'The White Hart was chosen for its central location, convenient for travel from all parts of London, the delicious Thai food and for its mural commemorating Martha Tabram's murder. For the uninitiated, we are in one of London's famous Jack the Ripper pubs.'

The Hoover building was the second item on the agenda. I stood up to address my fellow historians: 'I'm disgusted. If the tower block is built it will overshadow the view of the iconic building … We in Ealing have submitted our opposition. To challenge the monstrosity, you'll need to use the planning application portal on the Ealing Council's website.'

A Q&A followed. The third question put to me bled into a general discussion; someone mentioning work on the Troxy on Commercial Road. The chairwoman called us to order and a plan of opposition to the tower beside the Hoover Building was drawn up. I was to circulate Ealing's submission – mainly Tim Brody's hard work. A number of the other London groups had agreed to use it as the basis for their own submissions.

Several other items on the agenda followed. The longest discussion was about the things the London Historians should focus on going forward. At the end, we choose the pub venue for the next meeting: Shakespeare's local The George.

Much real ale was drunk that night. I had three pints: Two is careful. Four's too much.

At 10:30pm, I started my journey home at the new Whitechapel station. There is not much left of the old station, just the entrance front wall. I looked for, but didn't see, any of the old arched Art Deco window-frames. It is not progress if the construction of the new destroys the best of the past. The chrome, glass and bare walls have given it a feeling of space. I expected these walls to act as an echo chamber – they didn't. The purple 'Elizabeth Line' branding was visible all around. I approve of the purple roundels – the new aligned with the old.

I boarded my train and sat down on the end seat nearest the doors. As it was late and as I'd had a drink, or three to be more precise, I dozed.

Two men got on at Farringdon. They talked by the doors in the centre of the carriage. One of them had his back to me and held the overhead rail in his left hand.

Tottenham Court Road was next. I thought about the thirty-four-storey Centre Point above our heads: Grade II listed and described by Pevsner as 'coarse in the extreme'. The train pulled into the station. Doors opened and closed.

Before starting up again the train jolted and the man with his back to me stumbled backwards on to my foot – without an apology. I looked angrily at his back: he was about six-foot tall and wearing a dirty white Aertex shirt and long shorts that showed off hairy legs. He had pulled-up woolly socks. These clothes suggested he might have just been climbing a mountain. I didn't like him. His build and lack of manners suggested a bloody rugby player, his physical presence, maybe army?

As the train started to go forward, he stumbled back again and trod on my foot again! I was pissed off now. Who the bloody hell does he think he is? I wanted to snort and hiss to let him know my discomfort, but being in a public place I did nothing.

A couple got off at Bond Street but, oh no, he didn't get out of their way to let them pass by. He moved his hand slightly upwards but kept a firm grip on the bar above his head. The couple had to pass underneath his arm!

At the next stop, Paddington, I saw why he stooped with unease as his friend helped him off the train. For the whole journey, he had been holding in his right hand a folded up white stick – it was not what I expected.

But then again, you don't expect, down on the south coast, outside Ovingdean, the Blind Veterans centre and that is an Art Deco gem.

28. ROUTEMASTER

At Oxford Circus, I boarded a 159 red double-decker going south, towards Streatham station.

If I am in London for morning service at the West End Synagogue, I enjoy spending a little time on the buses afterwards. I've loved them for years, ever since I first followed a rabbi in a hat who almost fell as she jumped from the rear platform of a Routemaster.

The classic Routemaster buses, with hop-on hop-off rear platforms, served this 159 route up until 2005. There is both freedom and danger from having the back end open. I have seen a schoolboy holding on to the pole at the back, jumping off, running behind the bus and then jumping back on. Seven thousand were built and served London for forty years. The most iconic London bus is the RM!

I'd wanted to try out one of the new pretend ones for ages. I heard all the names: the Bloat Bus; the Boris Bastard; the Roastmaster.

The bus that turned up resembled an old Routemaster but there were doors at the back and an Oyster card reader just inside.

The bus was busy; no space downstairs. I pressed my card against the reader until it gave out a reassuring beep to tell me I'd paid my fare and I went upstairs to find a seat.

There used to be smoking upstairs, can you believe that! The bus was full up there too. I was about to descend back down when a black TfL inspector said somewhat surly: 'You can wait standing here at the back.' I thought it good he was showing some flexibility; I knew nobody was meant to stand upstairs because of health and safety regulations. But shouldn't it be my choice if I want to kill myself? There is a balance to be struck between freedom and danger. I thanked the inspector. A little later he pointed out a seat and I sat down on it.

I found the bus far too hot. There was no breeze on the upper deck, no ventilation as the windows didn't open. No wonder the Roastmaster tag.

At Piccadilly Circus, a drunk man with his leg in a cast and a drunk woman in a dirty Burberry coat got on the bus. He must have had some difficulty getting up the stairs. They were both white skinned and drinking from cans of Kestrel Super. They looked mid-forties but acted like teenagers. The inspector watched them. The drunk man and woman disturbed several of the other passengers, particularly the couple sat directly behind them. The man in the cast had swivelled around and asked: 'Who has the darkest eyes, her or me? Her! No way.'

I read their aura; they had finished the previous night at St Thomas' hospital after falling down stairs while snogging; she had been protected by falling on top of him.

The inspector approached and asked them to touch a card to his card reader. He reminded me of one of the old conductors, but without the bulky metal ticket machine sitting on his chest and strapped around his neck.

The man said: 'No.'

'Either an Oyster card or credit card will do, sir.'

The drunk man ordered: 'Take our names and addresses, you have to, it's the law.'

The woman laughed.

The inspector told them: 'You have to pay your fares.'

The man and woman became louder and abusive. The man told the inspector: 'You wouldn't be like that to me if I was black.' The woman pointed at the man's cast. 'He's injured! He's only just got out of hospital'.

I decided to teach them a lesson. I whispered so only they could hear: 'Do you believe in God?'

The man looked around to try to see where the voice had come from: 'No!'

So, I transported the three of us off the bus without anybody else realising what happened. They were still holding on to their cans of Kestrel Super.

I told them: 'I think it's time for you to start!'

On transporting them back to their positions on the bus, my use of contracted time meant nobody else had even noticed their disappearance. They were transfixed by the experience. They put down their drinks and both quietly paid their fare.

I thought: There's a job well done.

*

Five years after I dealt with the situation on the 159, I was back in London for the funeral of the woman in a hat who had brought me much entertainment. How the men railed against her when she became a rabbi!

It was fun watching you crashing the boys' club! They called it 'a departure from Jewish tradition.'

Men can be so pompous quoting from this or that text: 'The Talmud states that women cannot be judges.'

'What about Deborah?' you asked. Fair play, challenge the sexists.

'Deborah is an exception and she did not judge disputes herself ... The Torah clearly prohibits a woman from judging.'

You argued with what they called a 'transgressive narrative' and their best counter argument was 'male and female minds operate differently.'

Their denials increasingly made me laugh. 'I am in no way suggesting a woman is not an excellent source of wisdom and counsel.' Hilarious!

After the funeral, I rewarded myself with a bus journey.

Back doing a round on the 159, I came across the couple again. I had exited the back doors and there they were aggressively evangelising at the bus stop. They called it 'recruiting' as they handed out 'free of charge' literature: *Watchtower* magazines and biblical leaflets.

Yes, they were reformed characters – no drinking, no swearing.

But, standing in front of a Jehovah's Witnesses' sign at the top of a literature display cart, they lay down the law to everyone who would listen. No evolution. The end is near. Only they, the chosen, would live on. No blood transfusions.

I considered intervening again.

The sober man, without cast or can of Kestrel, pronounced on how people should live their lives and quoted Proverbs from the Bible: 'A prudent person foresees danger and takes precautions.' It took me back to thinking about the dangers of freedom without limits.

I decided against intervening. In retrospect, it hadn't been a job done well.

29. TAKEAWAY FOREVER LIFE

7.51 in the morning and the DLR, crowded as usual, made its way to Canary Wharf.

The DLR has been all right today, so far. There are frequent delays as it relies on signals, points and wiring laid last century. The people are noisy. It is hot in the carriage, no air con, so I take off my suit jacket and put it on my knees.

I sip a little Sci-Mx. She once said of the Sci-Mx: 'You look like you are drinking rice pudding from a giant babies' drinking cup'. I know it makes me lean and strong.

As a young man, my cheeks were fleshy like a baby's – nothing unusual about that – but also nothing attractive. I had freedom back in those days.

I glance at my watch. My hand is pale. It's 7.53. Soon I will have to book up to go and top up my tan. I turn up the music on my Mobi to blank out the surrounding sounds. I want to think about the past. I need to concentrate. I need to understand. With understanding comes options, right?

Back at the start to our relationship I'd liked to 'slum it', looking for those elusive peak experiences. 'The flower has its roots in earth and manure,' who said that?

I'd been out drinking after doing an 'eight-hour' managing the distribution centre. I was staggering home, I felt tired and slowed to rummage in my bag for Pro Plus. I was all out. I scanned the street for a pharmacist – not in this neighbourhood. A takeaway owner dropped a red plastic sack – commercial waste – outside his shop beside a cardboard box. There was a muffled bang as a bottle inside the bag hit the pavement. 'Boneless Banquet' was written large on the side of the cardboard box.

I didn't want a hangover so I needed greasy food and entered the shop. I ate a salty kebab in the brightly lit and colourful plastic interior. Once finished, I went into the Shop 'n' Save next door to buy something to drink.

I returned to the street. As I walked on, I swigged from a 284ml carton of Elmlea Single Light – at the time I thought a cream substitute would be more healthy than the real thing, how stupid I once was. The multi-coloured neon drew me in.

It was as I moved down the High Street that, from a distance, I passed a closed 'Compare the odds' shop and saw the green neon sign glowing: Virgin.

I never enjoy riding the DLR: It's too old. It's too crowded. It feels like a transport vehicle, built from a child toy set, to venture into a 'Gotham city'.

I drink deeply Sci-Mx out of its see-through bottle and think about how everyone had told me: 'She's not suitable. Find someone else.' But I had wanted her for her nice texture and feel. I'd wanted the sweets that she offered. I'd needed her to live with me.

To approach I had to pass thru' a turnstile by making a 'donation'. Up close, I saw Mary, not that I knew her name then, enclosed inside a glass sterile cubicle, visible to all like some Amsterdam prostitute. She was cleaning one after another of her objects.

As I took in the view, I took a handkerchief from my pocket and blew my nose. I realized I wanted to distract her from the material objects. I wanted her full attention.

Up close, I spat on to the glass then put my lips into the spittle and smeared it all around the window. My saliva contained traces of grease and kebab fat.

She wiped with a J-cloth at the new mark but to no effect. She was putting on an act for me. From a cupboard, she took a chemical cleaner and a new cloth. She scrubbed to remove the spit but it was on the outside.

I stood there and thought: The boy watches the girl. She performs. The boy watches the girl …

The DLR emptied at Canary Wharf. The standing got off. The seated stood up and got off. The masses always follow the mass, right? I drink to the dregs of the bottle. I am out of Sci-Mx but I know ways to get more.

The girl? What did I do?

I ignored everyone and listened to my own heart. A real man does what he wants to do, doesn't he?

I knew I had to entice her with a good offer. I dangled the prospect of a materially comfortable life in front of her. I wanted her to chase it. She didn't. Mary came to me in a calm and resigned manner. Mary, named after the discredited virgin.

The train pulls into Deptford Bridge Station and I disembark. I walk as if I am the young man I was back then, towards that very street where I first saw Mary. It seems a different place in daylight.

It is funny how when you get what you want it isn't ever as you expected. Even though she isn't some fancy 'pure breed' she can be fussy. She told me she wouldn't have come with me if I hadn't been tall enough. When she stretches out with me and our bodies mingle, I know why. Yesterday, I commented on how great her muscle tone was 'for her age'. She didn't like that one bit. You shouldn't comment on a woman's age. Shouldn't comment on anyone's age, really. There's a playfulness about the way we relate to each other, so it didn't matter.

Yes, I was right to go with my gut instinct. It's worked out for us just fine. We have grown together. I have become decently frayed and we can satisfy our urges to our hearts' content.

As I walk down the High Street, I see the neon flickering off in the distance. I still feel its pull. I'm still drawn towards the possibility of new peak experiences. There are new models in new windows. I ignore them. I'm just here to pay my monthly instalment and, if I'm lucky, top up on Sci-Mx.

The forever life suits us. We have no other options.

30. FUNNYMAN

She'd written to Pat from Australia and now she was here, in his office, with a look that made him uncomfortable.

'Call me Joan,' she said, but so far she had not smiled once, nor taken up his offer of a drink. All she wanted was 'Tell me the full story ...'

'It's a funny old world.' Pat lifted his blue mug and took a swig of warm tea. He carefully placed the mug to the right hand side of his desk. 'Jack Finch was just another one of the lads at Terry Mortimer (Reuse & Recycle to Remove). Then his headaches started.' He picked up and tapped the second-hand wooden desk he was sitting behind with a stubby pencil as he looked directly at Joan for a response. He was fidgeting; he put the pencil down and crossed his hands.

Joan didn't say a word. She held her black leather handbag tightly in her lap. He could see the shelf behind her was grey with dust; he should have cleaned up thoroughly before her arrival.

Reluctantly, he continued: 'His head was giving him gyp as soon as we returned to the depot with the table, so Jack took a couple of paracetamol. Midday, he was still complaining that he was in pain so I suggested he take another two paracetamol. I shouldn't have, I know you're meant to wait a full four hours, but he was going on and on that it was real bad! Even after taking them, Jack complained to everyone about the noises in his head: "A repeating and sickening laughter." He tried to explain what it was like by comparing it to: "One of those laughing boxes. You know from a joke shop." …'

Pat had picked up the pencil again, without noticing what he was doing. He recognised it as the lucky betting shop pencil he had used to correctly predict Chelsea wining 2-0; he felt his luck had run out. He put it down on the desk again. He would have liked to have stopped talking but he knew Joan wanted to know exactly what happened.

'All the weird talk generated at base didn't help get the jobs done one bit.' He lifted his blue mug, drank a little tea and put the mug down. 'Tel was out and about, so as foreman I was in charge. I decided I had to give Jack the rest of the day off – he had started to disturb the other lads. I told him, "Go on home – you need a rest." I watched him pack up and leave with all his tools.' He paused. 'How was I to know Tuesdays were the days his missus and your cousin got together?'

He felt she was watching him; Pat shifted uncomfortably in his seat.

'If I'd have known …' He pulled an incredulous face; Joan remained silent; Pat felt he had to continue. 'Jack went home and as you know he found them in the marital bed … At the trial the police described the scene, concluding Jack must have been in a fit of rage. I still struggle with it; he strangled his wife Mary and crushed her lover's ... sorry, your cousin, Terry's ... head in with a hammer.' Pat shook his head. 'It's hard to believe the neighbours claim to have heard nothing.'

Pat looked at Joan again. He couldn't tell what she was thinking or feeling about what she had heard so far. There were marks in the leather of her handbag where her fingers had pressed in. A faint stale smell reached him. He noticed the wall holding the shelf was worn; the yellowish brick needed work, it exuded damp. He wanted to stop recounting what happened but knew he had to tell her everything.

'Thinking back, to first thing that Tuesday morning, I arrived at the depot with the van to see Jack prying nails out of an old chest of drawers with the back of his hammer ...' Pat felt he had said the wrong thing in mentioning that hammer again. 'Anyway, it was just like any other January morning, if not better than most. All there was in the sky was a few white clouds within blue. Things went strange on the way to the first job.'

He reached for his tea, for comfort; it's meant to be the best drink of the day! Putting the Chelsea mug to his lips set off in his mind: blue is the colour; football is the game! The tea was lukewarm; that's an awful shame. He put the mug down.

'I haven't told you enough about the business. We were doing more than all right before the ... We were making money. We'd installed a good work ethic and Terry had even come up with a new slogan: "We're Game for it!" ... When it happened, of course, the lads were shaken up ... We all were ... I even took a couple of days sick leave ... It's a good workforce. They asked me to ask you ... I'm starting to babble, aren't I? ... They wanted to know about job security. The slump wasn't their fault.'

Joan didn't move a muscle. He wondered whether she would utter a single word until he'd got to the end of the story.

'The full story, yes ... Jack and I were in the van. It was about 8.45. We were to pick up a second-hand table in Camberwell. I drove past Oval and then pulled up at a set of lights ... A man crossed the road in front of the van. The stranger's overcoat, jeans and shoes were all black, his scarf white and blood red. On first glance, I assumed he was a goth who had been out all night; you know, like that singer in The Cure with white powder on his face and maybe a smear of lipstick across his lips, but no. The greyness of his skin was real. Maybe he'd only just got out of bed as his hair was all over the place. The downward turned smile and heavy eyes made him look real sad ... The lights changed to red and amber. Jack shouted "Oi!" at the stranger. There was a faint delayed echo as the stranger turned to look at Jack. Jack pointed directly back at the man and called out: "Yes, You!" Then with a big grin on his face he shouted: "It might never happen." The man looked at Jack. Jack added: "Or it could be worse than you thought!" The man didn't move. He continued to stare blankly back at Jack. Jack pursed his lips and stuck his tongue out.'

He took a deep breath in. He felt damp from sweat on his forehead. He breathed out. She shifted slightly in her seat but remained silent – she gave no indication that he should stop. Joan was one cool customer. He took a dirty hanky from his pocket and mopped his brow.

Pat knew he had to finish recounting what had happened. 'Without any change of expression, and with slow movements, the stranger pulled a playing card from his coat pocket. The man was even slower as he displayed the card towards us. It was the joker. To be honest, I was concentrating on the road; the lights were about to go green. The stranger slowly put the card back into his pocket. He walked on silently. That's when I heard a whimper from Jack. I didn't check on him immediately as I needed to drive on. Down the road, I asked: "What was that all about?" All he said was: "Pat ... Pat ...I saw my own face in that card." I turned to look at him. He'd gone as white as a sheet.'

There were a few seconds of silence in the room. Pat brought his words back to the business: 'After Terry's death, our biggest problem was the publicity. We were in the national papers. Can't keep that sort of thing out of the tabloids ... The business became a pariah. Less goods coming our way was a real problem. But time heals. Or should I say people forget quick, don't they? Recycling is all the rage now. The depot is at a record level of turnover. We are back in profit.'

Joan said: 'OK. I have come to my decision ... I want you to rebrand the business Joan Mortimer (Reuse & Recycle to Remove). Use green in the colouring to appeal to the eco crowd. We can leave the slogan "We're Game for it!" as it is.'

'Yes, Ma'am I can get to the rebrand right away.'

'You can call me Joan. I'd prefer that.'

'Yes … Joan.'

'On the issue of staff … I don't want Jack Finch ever to come anywhere near the depot ever again, is that understood?'

'Oh, Jack won't ever be returning —'

Joan waited.

'Even though it was classified a crime of passion at the trial he was sentenced to serve twenty-five years.'

'He must *never* come back.'

'Ma'am, sorry Joan, no need to worry on that score. I've been to Crowthorne; visited him at his secure hospital … They run a strict regime; they don't allow him playing cards, shaving equipment or a mirror in his cell. The visitor suite was split using a Perspex screen. We talked through an intercom. He told me three times in a row: "When not on medication I still hear the laughter." … He's never getting out!'

31. SERVING KATE

The master and mistress could sack me at their will, but they like me. I have been with them for more than thirty years, since my mother brought me here from our village as a child. No one has ever called me pig girl here, the village children were cruel in their taunts. This household is so refined and well disposed. I wish I could be as good as them. I feel clumsy in their presence.

This morning, brioche was given to the guests, as a special breakfast. I cast a spell that Kate would not be hungry. I watched her; she ate nothing. The spell either worked or had been unnecessary. Kate rarely eats much breakfast and on this special day she might not have had much of an appetite. The left-over brioche was passed down to us servants. It was unusual not to be eating stale bread. The brioche was young, moist and sweet.

I was reminded, I left my aches and grey hair behind when I dreamt last night: *I unpinned red hair from its bun and let it cascade shiny and wild around my shoulders. I was young, my body strong but feminine. Light made my close-fitting lilac dress see-through. David was amorous. He admired my fine thighs and bosom. It was our wedding day. I, rather than Kate, would marry David. Everything they were meant to have, we would have.* I didn't sleep properly. I awoke as I have difficulty breathing.

My mouth is still sweet with a taste of brioche.

I've known Kate since the day she was born to the mistress. Look at her now, a woman. With her soft almond skin, her petite nose and chestnut eyes, full of affection for David. No one could be more beautiful.

She has everything. Her room is spacious and has a big window that overlooks the garden. The high ceiling has a decorative rose and fancy cornicing. There is an ottoman to the left of the bed. There is even a fireplace.

I stand behind her. I can smell the new silk of her long white dress – the skirt goes everywhere. But that bodice needs to be tighter.

'Breathe in Miss Kate.'

Her mother had suggested a diet but nothing came of it. Not that David would care – he is so in love; he is a decent man. The only decent man.

Through the open windows the air carries a waft of honeysuckle and the smell of pork roasting. My mouth waters in anticipation of the lunchtime feast. I have always found it difficult to maintain a healthy weight. I fear failure. All my family were big people, with hearty appetites. My mother once tried to starve me. That failed. I know I need to act. I am a sinner who requires drastic punishment. I have been able to do intermittent fasting – I make more sacrifice at Lent – the weight drops off. But after, the weight always returns. What can you do when you crave to eat?

Miss Kate is far from fat. I pull the strings tighter.

'It will be madam tomorrow!' says Kate. Then salt tears fall from her heavily made-up eyes and across her powdered cheeks.

'Oh, don't cry.'

'I'm so happy.' That is all Kate says.

'There, there, Miss Kate.'

Bells rang out as if calling for the bride to come quickly. There is a rap on the door from the master telling us to hurry.

'Five minutes.' I call out. I knew Kate would not be happy until I had redone her make-up before pulling down her veil.

*

I hobble into the church and tell myself to sit near the back. I knew that during the service I would be able to slip out, unnoticed.

Halfway through, everyone was singing. I hold on to a roll of my fleshy pink waistline, I let go and look around. It is time. I slip out the back of the church. Walking, after kneeling, my knees shout out in pain.

I had chosen my time well, there is nobody to be seen as I walk through the hall to where the wedding presents are stacked neatly in a tall pile on the piano.

Kate and David are so happy today – shouldn't the happiness be shared out?

There is one wedding present I want for myself – a miniature silver box so dainty with the engraving of a pig on its lid. There are six little boxes in all, each with a different farmyard animal on the top. There it is – the fat pig quizzically sniffing at things on the ground in front of it. Surely, they wouldn't miss one. I look around again, I'm afraid I might be caught. What then? I look again at the boxes and pocket the pig.

I walk back towards the church past tables laden with fancy dishes, silver cutlery and fine glasses. I return to the back aisle and think again about the dream I had. When I awoke, I was crying, knowing I am an old spinster and would be staying that way. My mother always told me not to get ideas above my station – my one purpose is to serve.

If only Kate was gone and I could put an aphrodisiac in David's wine. At least then he would look at me and see an attractive woman. I could hold my head upright as I talked to him. And, I would keep on giving David the love draught until he was tongue-tied and frightened by his feelings for me. But I have no aphrodisiac.

When the service ended, the smell of the pork is thick in the air. Before the big feast, I return to my room, part of the servant quarters at the very top of the mansion.

I've started to struggle to climb the stairs without gasping. My room is box-shaped, apart from the sloping ceiling. It is undecorated. Furniture is sparse; I have my cot and there is a chest of drawers for my clothes. If I was to complain I'd say the room's too narrow, it can get freezing in winter and there is an ugly pipe going in and out of the wall near the door. But it's clean – I like to keep it that way. And, there is little light, as there is no window; this suits me as I like the darker realm.

I reach into my pocket and take out the little silver box – a part of them! I will hold on to the cot to get down on my knees so I can hide it in a hole behind the skirting. The box is my talisman. I will cast spells over this marriage.

One day Kate will be dead and the pig woman will be young and lithe again.

32. I DIDN'T RECOGNISE HIM

It is my turn to accompany Molly to Saturday morning school.

On the high street, I see tables and chairs already outside my local coffee shop. I look at my watch: It's 8:45am. The shop's formal opening hours are 9am-7pm but, I know, the shop can open at any time in the hour before 9am. The owner must have woken up early today. Feeling blurry, I deviate towards the attractive prospect of a cup of coffee.

I push against the glass panelled door and behind me a male voice says a friendly 'Hello.' I don't know if this greeting is to me, to Molly, to both of us or to someone else.

Before I have time to reply, or even think, he asks: 'You're not working today?'

I now assume I'm being addressed so I turn towards the voice. I can feel Molly's presence close behind me. From the doorway, I scrutinise a tall, black man, wearing a blue boiler suit, standing on the pavement. His middle-age is shown in a greying beard. Why don't I know this guy? He's not an old school friend or anyone I've worked with. He seems to know me. I don't have a famous face. I respond: 'Hello … No, not working today.'

'Can you buy me a coffee?' He puts his right hand out, there is a multi-thread bracelet on his wrist.

'No,' I am abrupt.

I lead Molly inside the coffee shop.

After being served, we take my Americano and her Coca-Cola outside to sit at a table in the sunshine. Molly piles three textbooks on the table then hitches her skirt upwards before sitting down.

The man has moved on down the high street. He is too far away to be able to see if he is asking other people to buy him coffee, or not. I wonder whether it is Molly that he knew. I could ask her? No. I did the right thing to protect her. There's a drugs and rehabilitation centre down the road, perhaps the man in the blue boiler suit came from there.

He reminded me of a guy Philip and I met in Belize. 'Benj' he called himself. He'd approached us as if he was our friend too and he'd worn one of those thread bracelets too.

I feel the two men are connected. They seem so similar. Full of charm and after something. Could they be the same person that had aged? No, that couldn't be. It's not possible.

Molly sucks up Coca-Cola from her can through a straw. Her eyes watch the passers-by. He pale legs jiggle.

My mind drifts back to Belize and that holiday in the '90s.

*

Philip and I were in Belize City. As we were backpacking,

we'd told ourselves: 'We're travellers not tourists.'

I wasn't feeling 100% as I had diarrhoea. We'd been to the Quay's and I'd nearly drowned. That had shaken me up or maybe I'd just picked up a bug from something I'd eaten.

We'd left our rucksacks at the hostel and were walking into the city. Philip wanted dinner, when the tall black man cycled past and greeted us warmly: 'Hello.'

We attempted to show no interest but he kept up trying to have a conversation with us: 'Call me Benj.' He followed us on his bike when we walked on.

He was persistent, chatty, friendly and not without charm. Benj recommended an 'excellent restaurant' he knew then pushed his bike as we walked to it.

Even though, I explained 'I have a stomach upset' I ate a meat dish with coconut rice. It wasn't 'excellent'. Benj tried to sell Philip a block of hash – the size of a family bar of chocolate. Philip told him we didn't want it. Benj gave us a couple of joints anyway. He handed them to me: 'Smoking marijuana will be good for your stomach.'

After eating, Benj took us to the side of a waterway busy with men drinking bottles of beer. Two of Benj's friends joined us, they didn't have any of Benj's charisma.

The waterside area began to empty as dusk approached.

Benj disappeared to 'fix my bike' and we were left with the two unfriendly men.

Looking around the waterside it was now empty. I felt

immediate danger and walked. Philip followed. The men followed Philip.

Luckily, directly around the first corner there was a bar. I went up to a group of four men and started talking to them. It seemed a whole lot safer talking to random strangers rather than the men we had been with. The two men persevered asking us to come back to the waterside for a drink. Instead, five minutes later, Philip and I headed towards the centre of town - to a touristic, busy, hotel bar. The two men followed.

About an hour later, in the town bar, the men became very aggressive and demanded money. They told us: 'We are police and know you have cannabis on you.' I immediately felt a burning sensation in my checks – I'd had this before at the start of a panic attack.

Philip asked to see identification. One had an official looking letter written in Spanish. The second said: 'Other police officers are on their way.' I didn't believe their story but that didn't stop me from becoming really sweaty under my armpits. To be on the safe side, I knew I had to dump the joints.

I wanted to wander away from these men again. But I couldn't wander off – I needed to protect Philip. I went to the toilet claiming diarrhoea and ditched the joints behind a cistern.

Twenty minutes later, the two men, not getting anywhere, left us in the bar. After a further half an hour, I returned to the toilet and retrieved one of the joints.

Back at our hostel, before bed, I smoked it. It did nothing to help my diarrhoea.

*

Another friendly: 'Hello' takes my mind away from Belize. An overweight black woman is going past us on the pavement. What's going on today!? Was this greeting to both of us, to Molly or to me?

I ask Molly in a flat voice. 'Do you know her?'

'Nah.'

'No. Me neither.'

Molly sighs as if I'd said the wrong thing then pulls a hand through her hair, messing it up on purpose. Before I'm able to pass comment, she says: 'Can you buy me a new backpack?'

'Yes, I know, dear.' Her last bag split – she'd been stuffing it too full with school books. 'Maybe when we finish up these drinks ...'

A few quiet minutes pass and the overweight black woman, now carrying bottles of clothes washing liquid, walks back past us. We nod at each other. She is not unattractive. I think I do know her; she might work at the salon where I get my hair cut.

I'm low on cash but I know there is a discount 'outdoor speciality shop' on the high street that seems to sell everything. I'm intrigued; maybe I can find a low-cost backpack there?

'Let's get this backpack of yours!' I stand up. Molly picks up her book.

At the front of the 'outdoor speciality shop', Molly waves, with her free hand, towards an Asian boy in the booth selling mobile phones. I'm annoyed; her hair is disarrayed and she is wearing her clothes in the way the school disapproves.

Why am I so annoyed? Perhaps it's thinking about that Belize memory. I still feel anger towards those men. Benj probably wasn't even his real name!

We go inside. There is a gold lamp on the front counter that the shopkeeper hasn't got around to putting it back into storage. I ask: 'Do you sell backpacks?'

The shopkeeper doesn't look at me directly. 'Yes, at the back beside the camp beds.' I assume he never looks directly at any potential customers as he doesn't want to embarrass or maybe put them off. Perhaps he needs the young lad at the front, here inside the shop, to help him actively sell.

We follow a sign saying: Camp Beds.

Behind a collection of camp beds in dusty canvas bags there is indeed a pile of cheap backpacks on a shelf. The shop is in need of a good deep clean, no wonder it is discount. I grab the bag on the top and read the label: Red backpack [41cm(H) x 30cm(W) x 15vcm(D)] with padded straps. It feels flimsy in my hands; as if it would fall apart after a couple of uses. Philip can buy her an expensive one next time.

I show Molly the bag. 'Will this do?' I didn't mean to sound aggressive. 'Happy with the colour?'

Her young eyes watch me. 'Yup.'

I return to the shopkeeper, Molly in tow. I put the backpack on the counter in front of him. Without talking, he rings up the price: £12.28.

I try the card reader but it doesn't work.

Molly bends her head downwards as she picks up a blue packet of extra gum.

I can see dirt. 'Don't touch the shelf … Put that down now.'

Molly puts the gum back on the shelf. 'I didn't do what you are saying.'

Even after I explain carefully, Molly is worried of catching more than 'sneeze germs.' I need to placate her. I assert the opposition of my earlier statement by saying: 'It'll build up your immune system, which is good.'

The shop keeper is staring at me directly to hurry me up. 'That'll be £12.28.'

The second time I try his card reader, I leave my hands in the air, as if pleading, as I wait for it to authorise the transaction. It is still no good.

I take a different credit card out of my card holder 'Third time lucky.' I reach out and touch grubby wooden wall panelling. 'With luck.'

It works.

I hand the backpack to Molly and she stuffs her books inside, zips up and slings it over her shoulders. On the way out, she waves towards the boy in the booth again. Even though I have one less chore to do I feel annoyed. Is it with her or is it with me?

I think back to the man in the blue boiler suit. Why didn't I buy him a coffee? I could have so easily bought him a coffee. But he wore a friendship bracelet just like Benj. A false flag to false friendship. Reacting in reverse to this lying symbol was the correct thing to do. Neither of them were my friend.

No, I'm not being 100% honest with myself. There is a simpler more selfish answer; I didn't buy him coffee because I just didn't want to create problems for myself.

33. DRINK, FOR TOMORROW WE DIE

It was raining. Jan held Madeleine's umbrella open over the two of them, gallantly. His other hand was around her shoulder. He leant over and kissed, then nibbled, her ear. *Things are going well.*

'I don't know Jan, we … we work together,' said Madeleine. 'I've got a reputation. We've got to be more careful. I don't want us to be seen.'

Sod the risks. We've sneaked around from too long. We are consenting adults. He moved his lips to hers and kissed her full on the mouth. He could taste wine and cherry. *When we snogged in the elevator, the possibility of being caught was a thrill.*

Jan had been told on numerous occasions don't mix work and romance. But he knew plenty who had dated, even a few who had married, from a work situation.

There's no stigma from meeting people via Tinder or other social media sites anymore. In comparison, an office romance feels old school.

'Oh, I'm getting all wet, this is —' said Madeleine.

'What about over there?' Jan pointed to a church on their left.

'Well …' pondered Madeleine. The church had seen better days. The large sign outside was broken – it read: 'St Peters of …' the last word or words lost.

'Come on,' he winked. Jan climbed a foot-high wall then held out a hand to Madeleine. She took the hand, followed and once over the low wall gave him an encouraging squeeze. He knew she liked his body, the time in the gym was well spent.

They walked arm-in-arm towards the grey main structure. Madeleine's heels had a tendency to sink into the ground, making walking difficult. He felt a dampness at the ankle of his trouser leg.

'Maybe I should throw my coat on the ground to stop your feet getting wet, like Sir Francis Drake?' he said.

'No, silly.' She laughed attractively.

The church was derelict. There were scaffold poles propping up walls.

Jan noticed an open door with steps downwards. 'Why don't we shelter for a moment in there.' *The further we go tonight the more I could get ahead. If it goes pear-shaped, yes, it'll be me that is 'redeployed' but that would suit me just fine. Might even get a pay-off.*

A dank smell emanated from the dark entrance, as they approached.

Madeleine was hesitant, 'I don't think we should …'

Jan silenced her resistance by pressing his body and lips against hers and pushing his tongue deep into her mouth. He felt ready to perform. He had been careful not to drink too much; he had kept to a total of four pints for before, during and after dinner. *All paid for on her expense account. I'm a kept man. The power dynamic is sexy.*

A light appeared, illuminating the entrance and down the stairs. Madeleine pulled away from Jan. 'What was that?'

Jan laughed: 'Let's go and have a look.'

'No Jan. I'm frightened.'

He rolled his head to one side and back, then took Madeleine's hand. He led her down moss-covered stairs; it seemed to get colder and damper each step down. At the bottom was a crypt – all the lights were on.

Jan saw the first spaces for coffins were empty. There didn't seem to be anybody, alive or dead, there. *Has it been desecrated? No, that's not the right word. Has it been deconsecrated?* He said: 'I don't see any body remains.'

She nudged him in the ribs. 'Silly.'

There was a rustling noise. Jan looked at Madeleine. She stepped backwards and, by accident, leant up against the damp wall. 'Egh it's creepy down here!'

He put his hands on to her shoulders. Moisture had passed on to her coat. *She might be my boss but she'll be great in the sack. Look at that purple lip gloss nearly all gone now.* He moved his hands to around her neck and kissed her deeply. The kiss went on and on until he heard a movement from the other end of the crypt.

They both froze. *She must have heard it too.*

Jan slowly turned around – he couldn't see anything. He moved forward, leaving Madeleine where she stood, and looked around a pillar. He saw a rusted cross, then edged towards where he thought he had heard the sound. In front of him he found two damaged coffins strewn with litter and graffitied with indistinguishable squiggles except for the name East 17. His hands were trembling.

He remembered Madeleine. He called out her name. There was no reply. He turned to run and there she was grinning at him.

'God, you gave me the willies. Why didn't you reply?'

'I don't know, let's get out of here.'

The lights went out. It was pitch black. They embraced in reflex; for reassurance. They were not alone in the crypt.

The faithful deceased would ensure there would be no sex for the out-of-wedlock that night.

34. MAGUS

In Madog's study, a black/brown collie slept in its dog basket. On his coat, black dominated, the brown was in patches giving a mongrel appearance, while he had white on his four paws providing him with an inappropriate cute look.

The sculpturer sat down at the desk, in front of his widest bookcase. Stacked, every which way, with books on esoteric themes and overflowing at the top. Merlin had suggested he tried to find a real woman to put in one of his art shows.

Madog wasn't satisfied as he hadn't been getting something he wanted in his love and sex life. Hope told him maybe he could find an exciting new partner. He couldn't stop himself putting pen to paper and writing the advert – even though he expected placing it into the personal ads was a doomed mission. His entry read: *Dionysian Magus throws out an opening spell to enchant witches. Scared to worship? Sex with magic? Tantra, tarot or therapy? Are you strong enough to resist my coven love? Or tell the truth to share the devil? Come to Baal.*

On paying the newspaper, he sighed: 'We're all addicts for the unobtainable.'

Madog's advert when printed was clearly positioned at the very top of the personal column.

What he hadn't expected was for people to approach him for health / spiritual guidance.

Marian sent him a long letter about her symptoms: aches, pains and fatigue. What most interested Madog was what she wrote about *looking for love and answers* so he suggested they meet up.

She came to him in Plumstead. At that first meeting, Marian said, 'I feel I am to blame for the failure of my marriage ... I was always a reserved person. Howard called me distant and then, at the end, cold.'

'Are you making the most of your new freedom?' Madog added: 'There are so many rich pleasures in life.'

'I don't deserve pleasure.'

'Could you unpack the 'I don't deserve pleasure' a bit? For yourself, going forward.'

She talked about herself for about a quarter of an hour before saying, 'I feel you are listening to me, reading my mind and influencing me.'

Madog looked at his watch, 'I have to talk to a gallery owner in twenty minutes ... Perhaps it would help if you gave quick thanks to all the teachers in your life.'

She happily complied.

As she was leaving, Marian said, 'I hadn't known what to expect when you opened the front door an hour ago. There was such a strong scent of old books. That's all I remember: lots and lots of books!' She added: 'Once I had seen your collection, I knew I had come to the right place.'

He replied proudly, 'It's the greatest collection of gnomic literature this side of Christendom.'

*

Madog thought Marian was pretty so he met her again but at her place the second time. To kick things off, he read her tarot cards. Marian said she enjoyed the spread of her cards, which had been mainly cups (he commented, 'representing all that is female in your life') and swords ('male').

He suggested carrying out Feng Shui on her apartment. Marian was unsure if the moving of pictures, mirrors, plants and furniture around was really necessary but she said: 'I'll give it a try.' He repositioned a painting of a seascape onto a different wall to give more balance to her living space, placed a hand mirror in the window, which followed the line of a road pointing at her flat (tongue-in-cheek he said 'it will reflect evil spirits') and in her bedroom moved the head of her bed away from a set of plugs so she didn't receive unnecessary electro-magnetic radiation while sleeping.

The next morning Marian sent him an email reporting that she had slept better.

*

A week later, Marian came again to Plumstead. Madog watched her closely, only half-listening to her words, as she described her symptoms in their fullest detail: 'Torpor and sadness comes with the back pain. Diarrhoea with emotional upset.' As she spoke, he saw her right hand covered her mouth except for her index finger which pointed to her left ear.

He diagnosed, 'Your illnesses are of a psychological nature so I`m going to prescribe a special homeopathic cure that can be traced back to the Celts. It`s an invisible cure for invisible illnesses.' He looked into her alluring eyes. 'In South West Wales there is an energy around the full moon. The moon brings out what civilisation suppresses – things hidden, strange, deemed mad, from our dark side ... This part of Wales resonates in the energy ... The fathers of our fathers, calling themselves Saxon, had a bloody war that overthrow the Celts. They moved into their lands but became consumed by the very culture that they had conquered. The ghosts of the dead from both sides still exert a wrathful energy that can support us today – if you can channel it.'

Her eyes widened.

To Madog, her black irises took on the form of deep pools of cool water. To push away any desire to enter the represented balm offered, he continued to talk. 'The Arthurian myths come out of South West Wales. The magic surrounding Merlin and Morgana and the love entwining Lancelot to Gweniver grew from this rich well ... If it is approached with an open heart – to destruction as well as creation – it can be a healing and positive place. But I warn you it will be purely destructive to those who cling to singular ideals.' Madog wasn`t really sure why he was telling Marian all this. He had put his Magus advert in the personal columns because he had wanted something for himself, not to help sort out other people's problems. He finished by saying: 'So that`s the prescription – a holiday at the next full moon in South West

Wales – for you to absorb the water, food, air and ambience.'

Madog went to the toilet leaving Marian with his books. He knew she would feel the trails all over his bookshelves, he had set them up a long time ago.

On his return, she told him she had decided 'there and then' to take up his suggestion.

'Good.' Madog went to his bookshelves in search for a particular book. On finding The Mabinogion, he carefully blew dust from the top before handing it to her. 'Some reading material for your travels.'

*

Marian returned from Wales with stories of visits to Arthur's Stone and Merlin's town Carmarthen. She handed back the book he had lent her, 'The stories were very interesting, rich in Celtic mythology.'

She was 'cured' of her illnesses, she said, but what replaced them was awe for Madog's powers. Through self-imposition, Marian made herself subordinate to do whatever he asked.

He found he enjoyed the feeling of power he gained over her. It turned him on. He suggested he cook for her and she accepted straight away. He prepared and they shared the five tantric foods. They ate fish, flesh and parched grain off white and blue china. They drank wine out of cut-glass goblets. The fifth course was sexual intercourse.

With consummation of their relationship, Madog knew Marian grew even closer to him. He told her to: 'Let your anger, pain and love towards all your ex-lovers, Howard, your parents and siblings be directed at, channelled towards, me. As if I was them, emotionally project onto me.' He knew, all therapists act in some form or other as gods. Through faith, the Magus knew he really could make magic flow. 'Faith can give strength!'

He hadn't directly asked her to but she began worshipping him.

*

Madog knew, at the very least, he should be honest if he was Marian's god. And, that there was sad humour in black truths. He sat Marian down to tell her his story: 'I have suffered no guilt since 2003 … It was on the South Bank of the Thames that I met Merlin. He introduced himself with three barks and nuzzled his long nose up against my leg. He was a collie with soft boiled eyes. I played with the attractive dog for a few minutes. But when I made my way home, the dog followed. I couldn't get rid of him. I checked the collar but there was no dog tag with contact details. For putting my hand out I was bitten and heard: *"Hello, Hello, Hello."* I thought I was going mad, hearing voices. But they continued, *"It's me, the dog, Merlin."* Merlin was here in my head but he was also sticking his tongue out and panting. *"I'm the magician who can improve your life hundreds of times over. All you have to do is think of yourself like a dog and let me be your leader. Like an invisible entity holding onto your lead."* I couldn't believe what I heard but felt powerless. As I didn't reply, assent was assumed … Merlin said, *"Come on boy! I name you Madog."* I didn't understand what this naming meant at the time. *"It's as if you are on the green grass on a cliff's edge. There is a sign post pointing over the edge but as a dog you, of course, wouldn't be able to read it. With me leading, you'll be able to walk on the air!"* I decided to see where this went, to try to follow Merlin. And as Madog I have found a new control over things. New powers! I've increasingly wanted to take part in sexual magic and live an extreme life. By the time, I had second thoughts, it was too late to go back. I was addicted to the Magus lifestyle ... You can be part of it, Marian ... Merlin told me to entitle my exhibition "A little bit of light worship." Madog always does what he is told.'

'Yes.' Marian simply said.

*

And, so, Merlin walked Madog who walked Marian, dressed in white and blue robes, towards the art gallery.

They arrived with plenty of time to spare. They walked straight past security guards and the crowd that had gathered outside pre-opening.

In the lobby, taking the place of a hat stand, was a statue of a naked man with handbags on each foot, hand and head. His penis was unerect and uncovered.

On the floor in the first room were the words 'Motherland and Fatherearth' written in huge letters. On top was a piece of art named 'Lesbians and Gays'. Twelve naked female forms were laid out to form a circle. The figures twisted at the waist. Each 'woman' was giving and receiving cunnilingus to the 'woman' behind and in front of her respectfully. In the centre of this ring was a column of eight male forms. One on top of another, they sat anally penetrated on each other's penises, like a stack of chairs.

In a second room was a Christ-like figure on his cross lying on the floor, a dominatrix encased top-to-toe in black rubber stood astride and directly above Jesus' face, in her outstretched right hand she held a whip, the end of which was playing with Christ's erect penis. There was a small crown of thorns around his balls.

Madog told Marian to sit and pleasure herself, on a small pedestal a foot away from Christ's outstretched right arm. She was meant to depict the Virgin Mary – humiliated and honoured. Madog left Marian as he had to deal with the press.

People entered the gallery space on the hour, at opening time.

Standing beside the word Motherland, Madog welcomed a critic from the Review of Modern Art. As Madog was asked about his process, he said, 'I formed each by slightly bending the sculpture. I was able to fit the female forms together like Lego blocks.'

The public watched him, as the artist. Madog knew, in the next room, Marian would be pleasuring herself, just as she had been told to do. She too would have an audience; people take the opportunity to be a voyeur where they can.

The next week, in the culture sections of the newspapers and magazines (including the Review of Modern Art) the exhibition was deemed: 'innovative', 'edgy', 'a success'.

*

Madog could now dominate Marian however he wished. She had given herself up to him completely. In fact, he knew he could do anything he pleased with her. He introduced sexual bondage and pain into her life, telling her: 'Go into your own masochism and be liberated onto a higher plane.'

The dark side of the magic left her feeling like a slave, no longer free to be without him.

He then invited her to his kitchen table and introduced her to the five nectars, force-feeding her blood, semen, urine, faeces and human flesh. As she lay on his white kitchen table, at the start, Marian told him she felt like a contestant on Celebrity Get Me Out of Here. While eating the faeces she called it 'gross' and grabbed her nose.

Madog took a covered bowl from his large double-doored fridge, removed cling-film, moved the meat it contained onto a white plastic chopping board then using a carving knife cut it into pieces. She didn't believe it when he told her, 'it's a slice of human loin', she simply pulled a face and chewed.

Afterwards, she felt internally stronger but more trapped and bonded to him. As she became more dependent on him, he felt less interest in her. She was his property now, like he was Merlin's.

*

Out dog walking, early one morning, Merlin had a new demand for Madog: *I want you to start murdering people. You have the power – nobody can stop you. You are a Magus – they are just Maggots. You deserve life being given up for you.'*

Madog found he was attracted to the idea and considered Marian as the potential first victim.

By the time he was back at his place, Madog had reconsidered. He had to be honest with himself. Being truthful, he was bored with her. She was clinging, needy and their relationship far too simple. He could ask her to sacrifice herself but he knew she would do it, so why bother?

The Magus was unsatisfied as he still wasn't getting something he wanted in his emotional life. He was even fed up of Merlin: *When was Merlin last original?* Together all three of them had become stuck.

Leaving was in everyone's best interests. *It's time for me to pack my bags and move on from both Marian and Merlin. Yes, drop both in at the deep end. Marian would have to get to know herself fast. It will be interesting to see if she survives. I hope she will. It's an experiment – giving her free will. As for Merlin, he will have to face up to not being so great – he's just a dog after all. If he wants people murdered, he'll have to do it himself.*

It's time for us all to grow up. I don`t care if Marian and Merlin end up hating me. I wish them well – I really do. I hope they don't end up hating all things of 'belief' – that's just a slow death from the inside.

For me? I'll settle in a new city. As he packed his bags, the Magus wondered about putting an advert into the small ads of the newspaper again. *No, I'll use a dating app next time.*

35. THEY ONLY WANT ONE THING

The sign outside the Brighton shop offered: Tarot card reading and crystal healing. A shop like this seems to me to be advertising magic and miracles; I have yet to experience this. But isn't it everyone's fantasy to go on a mystical journey? I was intrigued to find out what was going on inside. I want to see a real wonderland behind the glass frontage. I looked in and was disappointed to just see crystals and a selection of cakes. It was another vegetarian café.

As I turned away, I felt the first spits and spots of intermittent rain. I pulled up the collar on my coat. On hearing a pleasant tinkling noise by the door, I turned back. It came from a wind chime made of seashells. I admit, I said to myself: is that a sign? But the main reason I entered the café was because my throat was parched.

Inside, at the front, on the left-hand side was a large food counter. Beside the counter was a blackboard advertising carob coffee £2.50, herbal teas £1.95, flapjacks £2 and slice of olive oil cake £4.50.

On the right, was a 'Busy Bee Play Space'. A yellow sign with black writing read: 35 bee species are under threat – adopt the local Bee Action Plan. A petition, pinned up on the wall below, asked for signatures.

I was drawn to the five cakes on offer at the food counter. Two were uncut. All bar one were under glass domes. The fifth, sitting prominently on the counter, was a thick wedge of blueberry-coloured sponge with a white filling. The cakes for sale were wheat-free, dairy-free and organic. I considered a slice; but which cake would I choose? The filling looked whipped up from bean juice. I'd prefer proper cream.

I needed a drink and wondered if I could get a barley cup; I used to drink it as an alternative to coffee at night: 'Do you have a barley cup, without an excess of chicory?'

'No ... If you become a regular customer, we can get it in special,' said the white woman behind the till. She had beads in her hair; being in her early forties she really should've known better. This was no Joe Lyons with 'nippy' uniformed waitresses, serving tea and real cream cakes.

'Thanks, but I'm only passing through. I'll have a tea, *normal*, please.'

As I waited, I looked at a cork bulletin-board covered in

flyers and pinned cards advertising: Sunday Lunch Jazz at the Marina. Thursday 10am Hatha Yoga class at Brighton leisure centre. Taxis driven by women for women. Do you need a cat sitter? Do you need a dog walker?

The woman said: 'No need to wait. I'll bring the tea over to your table.'

'Great … Thanks.' I smiled, paid and walked towards an old armchair with a pink blanket thrown over its back. On the low table, a flower with open dark purple petals revealing a lush orange stamen, sat in an old third-pint milk bottle.

I sat back and casually look around to take the place in. I saw another blackboard but it was covered in weird writing and slightly supernatural symbols. There was a bookcase of exotic looking books; I could only make out the titles of a few of the bigger ones: *NLP for what you want*; *Cook Vegan for Good Health*; and, *Reiki for beginners*. On the top shelf was a Ouija board.

I wanted to study the smiling new-age hippies. What makes these people tick? They look happy enough bustling about in their jeans and woollen wear. There was an earth mother looking through a colouring book and two children in the Play Space: the little girl was wearing a red riding hood outfit; the boy a stripy jumper.

The customers' smiles reminded me of something else. Then it came to me: the born again. I wondered if these hippies thought they were above everyone else too. That's when I realised every single person in this café, including me, was white skinned. It reminded me of Lyn's wedding. Lyn was my best friend at school.

The day had started with a simple ceremony where Lyn and Stuart read their vows to each other standing in front of thirty friends and family. She became Mrs McKenna. There was a party afterwards. Up until near the end, the wedding was fun and loving. Late in the celebration, twelve white people, including the bride and groom, formed an African drumming circle. Lyn told me: 'The joy of the rhythm is innate in all human beings.' Watching the happy people drumming, I felt alienated. I had to bite my tongue. I was uncomfortable by the lack of ethnic diversity, and questions on cultural connection went through my head.

I watched the woman with the beads coming towards me. On a wooden tray she carried a small yellow-spotted bone china teapot and matching jug with extra hot water and tiny milk jug. There was a yellow cup, saucer, paper serviette and a yellow-handled teaspoon. All very dainty! Plus one metal strainer.

She placed the tray on the table in front of me and smiled: 'Organic honey from our own beehive is on the table, if you need to sweeten.' She pointed to a table close to the Busy Bee Play Space.

That old joke went through my head: I'm sweet enough already! I said: 'Thanks, I won't be needing that.'

The woman returned to her food counter.

I lifted the lid of the tea pot and looked in at the loose leaves.

I gave the contents a little stir. Using the strainer, I poured myself a cup – the tea was still too weak. I added milk anyway. The tea looked anaemic.

I sat back to let the tea in my cup cool and the tea in the pot brew. At the rear of the café were two doorways – one closed, one open. The closed door was a unisex, or should that be gender-neutral, toilet. There were fairy lights that blinked on and off around the open doorway and a beaded curtain tied to one side. Behind were stairs going downward. Beside the entrance was a stuck-up piece of A4 paper reading: Madame Yvonne. Tarot readings on Wednesday. Crystal Healing on Thursday.

Maybe I should start to dabble in the black arts? It's the tarot today. Lyn had her palm read before she got married; the palmist told her if she didn't change her diet she would be dead before she reached fifty. That would have been an alarming thing to have heard if Lyn hadn't already been fifty-four. I decided against having my fortune told.

I drank my tea. It was wet and warm but weak. I gave the tea in the pot another stir.

From my left, I heard a male voice quaver: 'Like religion you sacrifice yourself to an idea.' I lowered my spoon and turned around slowly. I didn't want anybody to notice I was putting myself into a better position to watch.

He was an older man, maybe six-foot, in a purple hemp shirt

and blue jeans, not my type, but he was still attractive – just about. What was interesting was that he was stroking his hand down the side of a girl's face as if to say *I love you*. To me, an observer, it looked more like he was saying *I own you*.

'Your health is number one!' The man voice was a little croaky.

The woman's voice was too quiet for me to hear her reply. They seemed to be in their own separate world. I wondered about her attraction … wanting to be led … a new father figure? I wondered if he was an anti-vaxxer … probably.

'It's a perfect circle, so they say,' said the man. 'It is what it is.'

What a ridiculous statement! Equally true to say: It isn't what it isn't. Except of course neither might be true if you are mistaken in the first place. Nobody can know everything. The strong are able to hold uncertainty. The weak strive for assurance to fill the gaps. The lost, craving certainty, are often offered false answers.

I didn't want to draw any attention so I returned to my tea, before shifting my chair ever so slightly. I was able to watch as they kissed and touched each other a lot more than your average couple would do. She was a pretty thing. He was what they used to call 'over attentive'.

An idea came to me. From my handbag, I took a notebook and pen. I sat back in my chair and wrote:

The Little Bee

In his work, the little bee buzzes towards the nectar, he knows nothing of the pollen. He is surrounded by huge white petals; above, below and on both sides. All around there are so many colours – in the light reflected off the white and in the shadows. The stamen bows ever so slightly on touch. Gold is freely given and collected. The bee buzzes out of the white world.

A girl comes to the hive to collect honey. She has on a red cape with a hood, for her protection. In defence of the hive, the little bee keeps watch. He follows the girl's actions, as she takes gold.

The bee did not sting the girl, that would have been his end. Instead, for his death, he goes back to his Queen and opens up his innards.

After a couple of minutes, I'd finished writing. I drank cool tea and pondered on what I had written, then put the notebook and pen away. I poured myself a new nicely brewed cup of tea. As I add milk, from my left, there was movement.

The couple got up to leave. He was closer to five foot eleven – not making six foot must be a disappointment. They put on coats. For the first time, I spotted he wore a bracelet of wooden beads – perhaps the Buddhist thing?

Before they moved towards the front of the café he held on to the back of her neck as if she needed controlling where she was going. I once called a hand like that the manifestation of a bully. I've heard it's called coercive control nowadays.

A test was needed. I took £20 from my purse and pushed it into my fist. As I stooped down, I saw a tarot card, the knight of swords, on the floor under a nearby table.

I stood up straight and opened my hand as if I had just found the note and held it up: 'Excuse me I think you dropped this.'

They both turned around; noticing me for the first time.

'As you got up, I saw you dropped this.' I offered the £20 note to the man.

He looked at me: 'I don't think —' There was that croak to his voice again.

'Yes, I clearly saw ...'

As he took the money from my outstretched hand, he held my gaze.

ACKNOWLEDEGMENTS

Love to Jo, my family and friends.

In writing this collection of stories I am grateful for valuable input from numerous sources: Carsten ten Brink suggested ways to improve most of the stories. Dr Jean Owen proposed 'guilt' as a theme. Robert Lentell, Judith Silk and Nicky Sullivan contributed ideas to some of the stories. Jo has helped with creative input. Many other people have supplied help and encouragement including numerous positive comments from Morley College writers.

I quote Rachel Carson, author of 'Silent Spring' (1962), in the story 'The planet has limits', and I would like to express my appreciation.

I'd like to add thanks to those involved in the creation and performance of the music that referred to in the stories: In 'I am not here' I refer to: (i) '(Theme from) The Monkees' written by Tommy Boyce and Bobby Hall; (ii) 'Happy Days' written by Norman Gimbel and Charles Fox; (iii) 'Poison Arrow' written by ABC; and, (iv) 'Fade to Grey' written by Visage. In 'Cool Britania' I refer to: (i) 'Burden of shame' written by UB40; and, (ii) 'Who Do You Think You Are' by the Spice Girls. In 'Men are so different, aren't they?' I refer to 'The Power of Love' by Frankie Goes To Hollywood.

Regarding the blurb, thanks go to: Jude for complimenting my writing skills; Brenda Kirsch for calling the stories 'very interesting' after carrying out a full proofread; and, Rachel Martin for her kind words in an early review.

There has been practical assistance from Molaheika Press to aid me pull together and publish this book.

I suffered a 'massive' (the actual medical term used) heart attack at the start of 2024 so I'd like to thank the cardiology team at the Hammersmith Hospital for their aid (a quadruple bypass) to my survival.

In the writing of the stories there has been recognition of trapped emotion, trauma, and associated baggage; and I acknowledge the expression of the stories may have loosened the load.

ABOUT THE AUTHOR

Henry lives in London and writes novels – yet to be published.

* Henry John Bewley's website https://henrybewley.wordpress.com/

* Sign up to his blog here https://henrybewley.wordpress.com/blog-2/

* Publisher: Molaheika Press https://molaheika.wordpress.com/

REVIEWING 'THE PENITENT'S ROSE'

Finally, the biggest thanks go to you, the reader. I hope you enjoyed my collection of short stories.

It would be greatly appreciated by me, and maybe the potential (or not) readers, if you reviewed this book.

Printed in Great Britain
by Amazon

40581951R00149